Horse Mad

Whispers

Kathy Helidoniotis

D1509038

WALRUS
BOOKS

Walrus Books, an imprint of Whitecap Books

This edition published in North America in 2010 by Whitecap Books. For more information contact Whitecap Books, at 351 Lynn Avenue, North Vancouver, BC, Canada V7J 2C4. Visit our website at www.whitecap.ca.

First published in English in Sydney, Australia by HarperCollins Publishers Australia Pty Limited in 2010. This edition is published by arrangement with HarperCollins Publishers Australia Pty Limited.

The Author has asserted their right to be identified as the Author of this work.

Library and Archives Canada Cataloguing in Publication

Helidoniotis, Kathy
    Horse mad whispers / Kathy Helidoniotis.

(Horse mad ; 7)
ISBN 978-1-77050-029-7

    1. Horses—Juvenile fiction. I. Title. II. Series: Helidoniotis, Kathy.
Horse mad series ; 7.

PZ7.H374Hox 2010   j823   C2010-904635-8

The publisher acknowledges the financial support of the Canada Council for the Arts, the British Columbia Arts Council, and the Government of Canada through the Canada Book Fund (CBF). Whitecap Books also acknowledges the financial support of the Province of British Columbia through the Book Publishing Tax Credit.

 Canada Council Conseil des Arts for the Arts du Canada BRITISH COLUMBIA ARTS COUNCIL

Printed in Canada by Friesens

10 11 12 13 14   5 4 3 2 1

*For Mariana, John, Simon,
Jamie and Monique
with all my love,
and for Seb
with all my heart.*

G'day mate!

This story takes place in Australia — so if you want to brush up on your Aussie slang (what are 'witches' hats'?), just flip to the helpful glossary at the back of the book!

one

The Nightmare

'Mum. Mum!'

I sat bolt upright in bed, the sound of my own voice echoing in my room. I was breathing hard. There was sweat on my forehead and my favourite nightie, the one that said *I ♥ Horses,* stuck damply to my chest.

I'd had it again. The nightmare.

It was always the same but never any less frightening. The black horse would scream, his hard body would lash and twist and his silver shoes would flash like a spotlight in my face, blinding me. I'd feel the terror and then the pain and then I'd be ripped from sleep in a tangle of sheets and sticky hair.

I squinted at my headless horse clock as the last pangs of fear ebbed away. It was 5:23 a.m. What Dad would call an 'ungodly hour'. I lay back into my pillow and rubbed at my neck.

'You okay?' Mum was at my door in her one-piece pink pyjamas. It looked like she was wearing a giant baby romper.

'Yeah,' I said, sighing. 'Same thing as last night.'

Mum crept into my room and sat on the edge of the bed. Her dark hair looked wild, like a hurricane had opened her bedroom window during the night, come inside and, ignoring everything else, torn across her head. She reached out and smoothed my hair back into place. 'They'll go away. Bad dreams always go away sooner or later.'

'How about more sooner and less later?' I grumbled foggily, rolling over onto my left, my favourite sleeping side. 'Sorry I woke you up again.'

'Part of being a mum, possum,' she said. 'Anyway, Jason's usually up partying at this time of night … well, morning. I've had to accept that broken sleep is my just desserts for everything I ever did to my parents when I was a kid.'

I could feel Mum smile in the semi-darkness and smiled myself, making a mental note to ask her exactly what that meant, at a decent hour that is. I loved that she would still do this for me. That even though I was twelve and a boarder at Linley Heights School, a very expensive private school that my parents could never have afforded if I hadn't won the riding scholarship, she would still wake up for me when I was at home. She'd still come into my room and sit beside me and wait until I fell back to sleep. I loved her so much.

Mum rested her hand on my head for a moment then stroked my hair. I closed my eyes wishing that it could always be like this. To always be here in my bed, in my room, and never have to grow up. I wanted to always be twelve and never too old for hair stroking. Public tousling was out — I'd made that clear on my first day of high school. I, Ashleigh Miller, was much much too old for tousling. But this stroking thing wasn't bad. It wasn't bad at all.

My best friend Becky Cho squinted down at me from under her riding helmet and gave me one of her most special smiles. She leaned forward in her saddle and patted her bay gelding's firm neck. Charlie, Becky's gorgeous part-Arab, tossed his head in delight. Charlie loved his mistress and she loved him right back. They'd been a team since Becky was seven. I'd often thought that they were the most perfect horse and rider pair I'd ever known, apart from me and my Honey horse, that is.

Honey was the best friend I'd ever had and I loved her more than anything. Home just wasn't home without her. Normally she'd have been in her paddock, in her cotton rug, nuzzling at my hand for a treat, but since Linley Heights School was a three-hour drive away I understood that my beautiful chestnut mare was happier where she was, and not being floated up and back between Shady Creek and Linley every few weeks. Now that she'd settled into her paddock at school and wasn't copping as many nips and kicks from the huge mare with the fly eyes, I didn't want to move her. I missed her so much it hurt, but she'd come home for long holidays.

'When're you going back to school?'

I shrugged, my hands shoved deep into the pockets of my jeans, and rubbed the toe of my jogger in the Miller Lodge (my family's bed and breakfast) driveway. The dry dirt rose in tiny clouds around my ankles, reminding me just how little rain had fallen in Shady Creek.

I wasn't used to having Becky so far off the

ground when we were talking. We were either face to face or side by side in the saddle. But for the first time in my life I was quite content on solid ground. There were plenty of horses to ride in Shady Creek and I'd vowed just a few weeks ago that I'd ride again. I'd wanted to so badly. Mrs McMurray, from Shady Trails Riding Ranch (my sometimes weekend workplace, second home and horse-paradise), would have given me a school horse for the weekend in a heartbeat. But there was a strange tight feeling in my chest now, where all the love and craziness I'd always had for horses had been. And with every nightmare, every echo of Lightning's screams, every drop of cold sweat that ran down my body in the middle of the night, the other feeling, the strange one, was growing. It was like it was eating away at my horse madness. The very thought made me sweat again. 'Soon. 'Bout a week I think.'

Becky scowled. 'Wish you'd change your mind about Riding Club. You hardly get to come to any meetings now that you're at boarding school. Today could be your last chance in ages.'

'I told you, Beck.' I sighed aloud, knowing I should have just told her how I felt straight up. I should have told them all. 'I don't wanna come.'

Becky rolled her eyes. 'But why? It just doesn't make any sense.'

'I just don't, okay?' I couldn't explain it to her. I didn't even want to. There was no way she could ever understand what was happening to me. She was just too horse mad to get it. 'I only just got back from physio and I'm tired.' That was true. Since the accident I'd had to do an hour of physiotherapy three times a week. I hated it. Sometimes it made me cry. But I knew it was physio now or misery later.

'But you've hardly ever missed a single meeting since you moved to Shady Creek. Remember your first day here? It was a Sunday, a Riding Club day, and you found Riding Club and Flea conned you into riding Scud and then you fell right in the—' Becky stopped suddenly, slapping her hand over her mouth. 'Sorry, Ash, I …'

'Don't worry about it.' I looked at the ground. I knew what everyone had been saying. (They had no idea, of course. No matter how old you get, some grown-ups think that you still go deaf the minute you walk out of the kitchen. They also think that you don't know how to pick up the phone extension upstairs.) I knew that my parents and the Chos had talked about me and that Becky had been told not to mention the accident anymore. (They thought that by not talking about it that my night terrors would disappear, but they hadn't.) And thinking about my first day in Shady Creek, the day we'd moved here from the city and I'd wound up being thrown from my creep next-door neighbour's psycho horse in front of every kid I was about to go to school with was almost too much. That day I'd earned my hated nickname, Spiller Miller, and had felt forced to prove myself as good a rider with as much right to live in Shady Creek as them. 'Doctors haven't given me the all clear yet, anyway.'

Becky gave me her sweetest smile. 'Pree's gonna be there.'

I arched one eyebrow, feeling a tug of temptation. 'Whaffor?' Pree was a committed member of Pinebark Ridge Riding Club, Shady Creek Riding Club's arch rival. But Beck and I both loved Pree (also known as Preezy-Boo, Preencess and Preety-Bops) like Romeo had loved Juliet. We were all sure it wouldn't turn out the same tragic way, though. In fact, we both were convinced that if Juliet had just taken an interest in horses and forgotten all about boys, she could have been saved. It had worked for Becky's older sister, Rachael, that was for sure.

Rediscovering her horsiness had saved her from the horrors of hormones.

'To see you, of course.' Becky wriggled in the saddle and looked over her shoulder at a small kid on a grey pony riding past the house in a glaringly new Shady Creek Riding Club shirt. Clubbers usually rode past my house. After all, the Shady Creek Riding Club grounds were at the end of my street. 'He must be new.'

'Why can't she just come and see me here?' I nodded towards the house. I hadn't left it much since I'd come home to recover from the accident. I'd liked it that way. In fact, since the nightmares started I'd liked it more and more. I hadn't even played with Toffee, my maniac miniature pony, as much as I should have. And he was as harmless as he was insane.

Becky bit at her bottom lip, just the way I do when I'm nervous. 'Ash, please! Just come for a bit. It's gonna be fun, I promise.'

'But I'm horseless!' I cried. 'What's the point of going to Riding Club without a horse?'

Becky shook her head, her dark eyes narrow. 'You never used to care. If it meant being with horses the old Ash'd be in it, ride or no ride. Don't you remember when you first came to Riding Club? You never had a horse then.'

'I'm still me, you know,' I snapped, but I knew she'd got me with that one. The old Ash would have done anything to be near a horse. The old Ash had collected horseshoes just to hold them and old brushes just to smell them and even pieces of trimmed hoof just because they'd once been part of a horse. The old Ash had hung around stables, covered her room in posters of horses and taken delight in mucking out poo. The old Ash had lived horses and breathed horses and dreamed horses and never felt like she was truly happy, truly herself unless she was on a horse's back.

But this new Ash didn't dream horses anymore. This Ash had nightmares.

Becky held out her hand. I took it. She squeezed my fingers. 'C'mon, Ash. For me.'

I smiled up at her.

'Well?' she asked. She looked into my eyes, hopeful.

I took a deep breath and nodded slowly. 'Okay. For you, okay.'

Becky grinned, her smile lighting up her face. 'Yes!'

As I walked to Riding Club, with Becky riding beside me, my tummy fizzed and bubbled and tumbled and my chest grew tighter. It was a strange feeling, yucky, uncomfortable. I'd had the tummy thing before, heaps of times. Before a show or on the first day back at school or after eating something that Dad had whipped up. But the chest thing, the tightness, was new and I had felt it a lot lately. After the accident I'd been okay, sore but okay. I'd decided to ride again and had been busting out of my boots to get back into the saddle. But then the nightmares had started out of the blue. I'd even had a few daymares, terrible moments of being wide awake and then, suddenly, being back *there* in that paddock, on my face in the dirt. I could see the horse and hear his screams and feel the pain all over again. My family knew about the nightmares — it was impossible not to know. But I hadn't told them anything about the day ones. I didn't want them to think I'd gone from being horse crazy to just plain old crazy!

'How's it going down there?' Becky said.

'No worries,' I said, wishing like mad I was telling the truth. I didn't feel a lot like talking, not with all those things with wings, flipping and flapping around inside my guts. So I shut up. I only hoped that Becky would do the same.

I hadn't walked to Riding Club for a long time. Since Honey had come into my life I'd only ever ridden down the road to the Shady Creek Riding Club grounds. I'd had so much fun there and learned so many things about riding and horses. I'd represented Riding Club in cross-country and won a four-week stay at Waratah Grove Riding Academy. I'd learned to ride Western at Riding Club. I'd made some incredible friends and I'd been coached by the most amazing riding instructor on the planet — Gary Cho, Western Rider extraordinaire and Becky's dad. Sure he told the worst jokes known to horsanity (some of which had seriously damaged Becky's emotional health) and Becky had suffered heaps at the hands of the Three Creepketeers (my next-door neighbour, Flea Fowler, Carly Barnes and Ryan Thomas, our mortal enemies) because they reckoned Becky got special treatment, but as a riding instructor Gary was the best!

Riding Club looked just the same. Gary's dilapidated office sat by the corral. The warm-up arena, large sand arena and cluster of trees where we wriggled on upturned milk crates during our club meetings lay behind it, and the cross-country course Gary had built with the help of some of the other parents still stood as proudly as I remembered it. I stared for a moment, taking it all in, rubbing at my arms.

'Itching to ride?' Becky said brightly, hopefully.

I glanced up at her and offered a half-smile, getting ready to tell another lie. 'For sure.'

Becky dismounted, but the wrong way — shaking her feet loose of her stirrups, throwing her right leg over Charlie's neck and sliding to the ground, both feet first. She pulled Charlie's reins over his sweet head and offered them to me. 'Corral him for me, will ya? I just wanna check something with Dad.'

Gary's gorgeous Pinto mare, Bonnie, was already in the corral, chewing thoughtfully at her haynet. Since Gary's return to Western riding they'd been inseparable.

I opened my mouth to protest, the yucky tight feeling in my chest nagging at me, louder and sharper than ever. But Becky was already gone.

I held Charlie's soft reins in my hands, looking at them for a moment. The last reins I'd held were Lightning's. I remembered the pain of them being ripped from my fingers, the silver-coloured buckle tearing at my palms as the stallion reared. A strange feeling began to wash through my body. It started in my feet and flooded into my veins, making my heart pump hard. I sweated, wanting to run and run and run, not understanding what was happening to me. Charlie nudged my arm as if to say, *Get on with it, Ashleigh. It'd be real nice to have my girth loosened a bit!*

I swallowed hard and tried to focus, telling myself I knew how to lead a horse. I'd done it hundreds of times. I stood on Charlie's near (left) side and held his reins underneath his chin in my right hand, taking up the slack with my left. I took a step forward.

'Walk on,' I said weakly, almost delirious with relief when he followed my command and took a step alongside me. What was wrong with me? I loved horses, I lived horses, I breathed, ate and slept horses. My first word had been 'pony'. And here I was shaking in my boots because a perfectly well-behaved horse was walking calmly by my side. I shook my head trying to get all the silly thoughts out and led Charlie into the corral.

I fought hard against the tingly feeling in my chest — the one that felt a lot like I'd just had a fright —

and tied one of the many pieces of orange twine hanging from the corral to Charlie's reins. If the gelding spooked, the twine would break before the reins did. I shortened the stirrup on his nearside, then walked behind him to his far (right) side, running my hand along his rump so that he would know exactly where I was, and shortened the other. The tingles were starting to fade, maybe because I was busy. I felt okay enough to wrap my arms around Charlie's neck and then buried my face in his mane, breathing in that sweet, familiar horsy smell.

'What's going on with me?' I whispered. 'What if they say I can't ride again? What about Honey? What will happen to her? What about Linley? Will they kick me out? And these nightmares — how can I make them stop?'

My throat went all tight and the first tears stung my eyes.

'You okay, Ash?'

I jumped away from Charlie, rubbing my eyes and nose on the back of my hand. 'Pree!'

Priyanka Prasad, one of my best friends and the best horsy joke teller in the known universe, grinned down at me from the back of her fat dun mare, Jasmine. Pree had the whitest, straightest teeth

I'd ever seen and, until she started Year Seven at Shady Creek and Districts High School, had worn her thick black hair in a plait all the way down to her waist. It was cropped to her shoulders now. Pree looked awesome but I didn't know if I'd ever get used to it.

Pree scrambled to the ground and threw her arms around my neck. 'It's so good to see you. Beck said she was gonna try and rope you into coming but neither of us thought you'd … I mean, we heard about your nightmares and … I mean …' Pree tucked her hair behind her ears and wrung her hands. 'Hey, have you ever heard this one? When do vampires like horse racing? When it's neck and neck! D'you get it? Necks and vampires?'

'Good one,' I said, forcing my face into a smile.

'C'mon, Ash,' Pree said, taking both my hands. 'You were okay before. You definitely decided you were going to ride again, didn't you?'

'Yes,' I said weakly.

'So what's happened?'

I shrugged and stared at the ground. How could I tell her? How could I explain? She was right. I had been all right before. But the nightmares, the daymares and the tingles were messing me up.

'Preezy-Boo!'

'Becks!'

I stood back and watched as my two best friends hugged each other, like I was watching two people I didn't know. It wasn't that they'd changed. I had.

They both turned to me.

'Well done on getting her here,' Pree said, holding up her hand for a high-five. Becky slapped her palm against Pree's. 'Only the magic of Mistress Cho could have produced such a happy ending!'

'Why, thank you,' Becky said, fluttering her eyelashes. 'Thank you very much.'

'Hey!' I snapped, anger boiling inside me. They were acting like out-of-control parents, talking about me as if I wasn't there. 'I'm right here, you know. And it's great to find out my two best friends have been talking about me behind my back. Why don't you just ask me what's going on? Why does everybody have to treat me like I'm some little baby? Why don't I go home? I hope you two are very, very happy together!'

I stormed out of the corral, completely throwing everything I had always known about yelling in front of horses to the wind. I didn't care anymore. They could take their horses and take their Riding

Club and …

'Ash!' Becky cried.

I stormed faster, so fast in fact I was practically drought-breaking.

'Ash!'

I broke into a run, my head down. I didn't know if it was even okay for me to be running, but I didn't care.

'Spiller Miller.'

I stopped dead. That voice. I looked up and found myself face to chest with a white mare. Her red-haired rider gave me a smile that would send shivers down a great white's spine.

'Carly.' I sighed. 'Still torturing Destiny, I see. Why don't you do something good for horsekind and drop dead?'

Carly Barnes, creepiest of the Creeps, widened her cat-like blue eyes, a sure sign she wanted nothing more than to string me up by my ankles from the nearest gum tree and set it on fire. She was flanked, as usual, by Flea Fowler, riding his revolting black gelding, Scud (the only horse I've ever truly hated), and Ryan Thomas on his huge of body and of heart grey gelding, Arnie. Ryan wasn't mean, just vacant, and earned his Creepketeer status by following Flea and Carly around and doing all the dumb things they told him to. Dumb things like terrorizing innocent twelve-year-old girls.

The Creepketeers had hated me from my first day in Shady Creek because I had come from the city and was befriended by Becky. I'd hoped that becoming tiny fish in a humungous piranha-filled pond at Shady Creek and Districts High would have mellowed them. I'd been totally wrong.

'Where's your mule?' Carly sneered. 'In the circus where it belongs?'

'Yeah, the flea circus,' Flea said. He cracked up laughing. Ryan thought for a moment and laughed along with him.

Just as I felt my fists curling into balls a familiar voice boomed over my shoulder.

two

Destiny's Fool

'A reunion — how nice!'

'Gary!' I smiled. Although I was furious with the Creeps and not happy at all with Becky and Pree, it still felt good to see him.

Gary Cho smiled back at me from underneath his tatty Shady Creek Riding Club hat. 'Everything okay here?' he said, his thumbs hooked over his belt, the one with the buckle so big it had its own gravitational pull.

I nodded, looking around to see Becky and Pree standing behind me. 'Yep.'

'Good to see you looking so well, Ash. You were still in a fair bit of pain last time I saw you.'

'Dad!' Becky hissed.

The Chos had been to see me while I was laid up in bed recovering. So had Mrs Mac, Mrs Flea, and even Mrs Adams from across the street. 'Yeah, I remember.'

Gary realized I was annoyed and grinned nervously. 'Help me with inspection? Just like the old days?'

I shrugged. 'Maybe.'

I was starting to feel a bit better. Maybe I'd overreacted at Becky and Pree. Maybe they hadn't meant for anything other than to get me out of the house and back into the horsy world. Maybe they'd been trying to do what best friends do for each other. Maybe I'd just needed to yell a little. I looked over my shoulder at them again. They were standing side by side looking at me, worry and guilt etched on their faces. I gave them a small wink, just to let them know it was over, and they beamed.

Carly rolled her eyes and pretended to vomit into Destiny's mane, then coughed like she had tuberculosis. I picked up the word 'loser' and wondered how it was that grown-ups went suddenly deaf in the face of pre-teen hostility.

'How about *yes*?' Gary gave me a smile and patted my shoulder.

I wrinkled up my nose, wanting to please him but too stubborn to say the word he wanted to hear at the same time.

'Okay then.' That was the best I could do.

'Great!' Gary headed back towards his office.

'Just like the old days, eh Spiller?' Carly spat. 'Heard you can't stay on a horse even with some posh riding scholarship.'

Flea cackled. 'They're wasting their money.' Scud tossed his horrible ugly head in agreement.

'Maybe you should be superglued to the saddle,' Carly said, a nasty smile tugging at the corners of her mouth. 'Or you could try Velcro.'

'Or they could tie her feet together, you know, under the saddle.' Flea was cracking himself up. Ryan looked from one Creep to the other, trying to get the joke.

I opened my mouth, ready to unleash every bad word I'd ever learned in my entire life.

'Ash! Front and centre,' Gary called. 'The rest of you lot — inspection!'

The Shady Creek riders lined up in age order: Under 10s first then Under 12s, Under 14s, Under 16s and finally Opens. I'd been an Under 12 for so long. Now I was an Under 14. Why did we have to get old? It freaked me right out.

Gary passed me a folder, the one he wrote down all his notes for inspection in. It was the same folder I'd held before I'd found Honey, before I'd even been a member of Shady Creek Riding Club. Inspection was the first and one of the most important events at a meeting day. Riders had to be well dressed in the correct uniform and safety gear, their horses had to be well groomed and all their tack had to be shipshape. Failure to meet Riding Club's very high standards could mean being barred until the rider got themselves and their tack up to scratch.

I followed Gary down the line of riders. The tingles were back. Stronger this time, like a thump, like my heart was beating harder than it had to. The new kid Becky and I had noticed that morning was first up for inspection. Gary admired his clean shirt but tightened his girth two notches. I made a note in the folder, concentrating harder on the pen and paper and writing as neatly as I could than on the boy and his horse.

We passed Sandra, whose severe allergy to horsehair, including that of her beloved dark brown gelding, Chocolate, kept her face buried in a box of tissues and away from most Riding Club meetings. She smiled and said, 'Hi,' and sneezed hugely into her riding gloves. The riders on either side of her groaned but Chocolate didn't even flinch.

'Ash!' A girl with a long bleached fringe and brown hair at the back, cropped as short as a boy's, beamed at me. She held her white riding helmet in one hand and the reins of a pony I recognized straightaway in the other. If that was Buttons, his rider had to be a Ferguson twin.

'Jodie?' I gasped. 'What happened? I mean, you look great, but … wow!'

Jodie clapped her hands in delight. I could usually only tell her apart from her identical twin sister, Julie, by the blue ribbon Jodie had always worn in her long brown hair. Now that she was in Year Six at Shady Creek Primary School she must have figured that she was way too old for colour-coded ribbons.

Julie bounced in the saddle. Boots, her cute bay Welsh Mountain pony, tossed his head in indignation. Julie's hair, and red ribbon, were intact.

'Ash! I can't believe it's you. It's like we haven't seen you for—'

'Ages, I mean we thought you'd never get home from that—'

'School, especially after what—'

I rubbed at my forehead. I didn't want to hear about it. I especially didn't want to talk about it. Not with them, not with anyone. Julie and Jodie had been my friends from my first day in the Creek. They'd stood up for me and helped me out and we'd ridden in the same team for Shady Creek Riding Club. But I needed someone, anyone, to get through a whole day with me and not mention the accident.

Gary cleared his throat and tapped Julie's saddle flap. She automatically moved her left leg back. He peeled back the saddle flap and checked the girth. Not only did he have to check that it was done up tight enough (but not too tight, of course), but that it was in top condition.

'Girth okay,' he said, running his hands over the stirrup leather. I gave *Girth* a tick in red pen beside Julie's name. 'This stirrup comfortable for you, Julie? Reckon it could go down a notch.'

Gary adjusted both stirrup leathers and Julie wriggled her bottom, smiling. 'Much better. I forgot to adjust them when I went up to Under Twelves.'

'You don't need to adjust stirrup leathers just because you go up an age group.' Gary rubbed

Boots's mane and the pony's head drooped in pleasure. 'Better to wait until you actually grow.'

'When're you coming back to Riding Club, Ash?' Jodie asked, her freckled face serious for a moment. She was mounted and ready to ride, looking cute as the button her pony was named after with her short short hair and helmet. 'You are coming back, aren't you?'

I stared very hard at the folder, wishing that I could suddenly vanish into the smudged and dusty pages. The tingly, thumping feeling in my chest swelled. Why did it seem that everyone was dying for me to get back in the saddle? Why couldn't they see that I needed more time? It wasn't just that my body wasn't ready — the doctors had made me understand that if I had another fall too soon I might never be able to ride again and there'd be plenty of other things I might not be able to do as well — my head wasn't ready either.

It was then that I realized I hadn't really talked to anyone about the accident. Maybe I should have. I mean, I'd told the doctors what had happened to me on the outside. But I hadn't said much at all about the inside. Mum and Dad knew I was having nightmares, but I hadn't said anything about the tingles. I didn't know what they were or what they meant. I didn't really want to. And I didn't want to make anyone worry even more than they already did.

'I have to go back to school soon, so it won't be for a while, I guess.'

'Oh.' Jodie looked deflated.

'Ash!' Gary called. I gave Jodie a quick grin and jogged after Gary, stoked for an excuse to get out of answering the question.

'Whaddya reckon, Ash? Would anyone at Linley Heights get away with boots like these?' Gary scowled at a pair of very scuffed black riding boots. I looked up at their owner. Carly glared down at me. Seeing her discomfort made me feel better, almost tingle-free for a moment. I waggled my finger at her behind Gary's back and shook my head slowly, like I'd never been so disappointed. Carly, like her horse, was usually immaculately groomed.

'Back to being folder girl, Spiller?' she hissed, once Gary had moved on to the next rider and was out of earshot. 'I can think of a few other jobs for you while you're down there.' She gestured to the neat pile of poo that Destiny had just produced.

'You know, if you'd just shut up there wouldn't be as much of that lying around,' I said, scribbling down a note about her boots. Suddenly I felt great, strong, in control. It was awesome.

Carly's face darkened and her mouth screwed up tight. 'I'll get you, Spiller. I swear I'll—'

'Next!' Gary boomed, making his way over to Jasmine and Pree. She was an honorary Creeker that day and had even thrown a blue Shady Creek Riding Club shirt on over her long-sleeved top.

'Hey, I'm sorry, you know. About before.' Pree's dark eyes were wide and she bit at her bottom lip as Gary moved to the next rider. 'We shouldn't have made you come if you didn't want to. It's just, well, we thought that maybe those dreams would go away if you could just see horses the way you used to.'

I sighed and stroked Jasmine's nose. 'I'll be okay, Pree. I'm sure I'll be okay again soon.'

Pree gave me a wink. 'I can't wait, Ash!'

I couldn't wait, either.

I sat on the corral fence watching as the Shady Creek riders warmed up their horses. I knew Gary's routine inside out. Walking around the arena in circles then moving into a trot for three or four laps. Up to a canter in circles, then serpentines or 'S' shapes, and then the whole thing over again in the opposite direction. The warm-up was a great way to get in touch with your horse, to feel them moving beneath you, to feel fused with them in body and in spirit.

I watched them, feeling like an outsider. I couldn't believe that I'd once been a part of this or that I ever could be again. I wrung my hands together, thinking about the money my parents had spent on my riding and how much the Linley uniforms had cost them and I started to sweat.

'Stop it,' I told myself aloud. I held tight to the rail, the tingles thickening, and jiggled one foot in the air then shook my hands hard and rubbed at my eyes. I opened them again — everything was blurry. I blinked it all away and refocussed on the horses and riders in the distance.

My eyes followed Becky and Charlie around the arena, drinking in the sight of my best friend and her beautiful bay horse. A year ago I wouldn't have noticed, but I knew Becky was talking to Charlie — her hands were speaking to him, her legs and seat were guiding him. Every now and then her lips moved and I knew she was praising him. The gelding's ears flicked back and forth. He was happy and alert, willing and gentle. The best horse out there. The very best.

Pree had managed a bumpy trot out of fat, round-as-a-barrel Jasmine. She was beaming with pride, throwing her head back every now and then to giggle.

I felt a nudge and jumped, clutching at my chest with one hand, fear surging through my body, and gripping the corral fence with the other.

'Gary!' I gasped. 'You scared me.' The throbbing began to settle, but my legs and arms ached from the rush of adrenalin.

Gary joined me on the fence. It wobbled a little. 'Hope this baby can hold us both up.'

I held a little tighter to the wooden rail. 'Wish I was out there. Sorta.'

Gary patted my back. 'You will be. When you're ready.'

I sighed. 'And when will that be? I mean, I know I wanna ride and I know I love my horse, but I feel so, so …' I looked up at the clouds, hoping to find the right words scrawled across the sky. 'Lost.'

'Horses have a habit of finding you, Ash,' Gary said. 'Whether you want to be found or not.'

I nodded, remembering how he hadn't ridden the whole time I'd known him until the Western show. He'd kept his past as a Western riding champion secret from Becky her whole life, and it hadn't been until Destiny had nearly died from the worst case of septicaemia that Shady Creek's incredible vet, Amanda Filano, had ever seen, that he'd finally filled her in. He'd lost a horse to a riding accident and never gotten over the hurt and the guilt. Now that he'd faced his demons he'd been able to get back in the saddle. Maybe the same thing would happen to me. I prayed hard to the horse gods that it wouldn't take a marriage, two kids and a nearly dead mare to bring me back to riding. I smiled to myself. The horse gods were my friends again.

We sat quietly for a moment, each of us lost in our thoughts. Finally Gary jumped down from the corral fence, landing on the dry earth with a loud *ooft*.

'Fancy doing another job for me?' He smiled, squinting into the sunlight.

'Like what?' As long as it didn't require beating my best time over the cross-country course, I'd be okay.

'Check out the cross-country fences for me? I was thinking of designing some new jumps and could use your expert advice.'

I rolled my eyes. 'I'm not an expert.'

Gary clutched his chest. 'You mean to tell me that watching you win the Waratah Grove Junior Cross-Country Riding Championship last year was an hallucination? I really need to get my medication checked.'

'That was a long time ago.'

'Seems like only yesterday.' Gary sniffed, fake-crying. 'I feel so old!'

I giggled. 'Fine, you win.'

'That's the girl.' He pulled a crumpled notepad and a pen from the back pocket of his jeans and pressed them into my hands. 'For your thoughts. You know, on the fences.'

I nodded.

Gary was one of those people who just knew when it was time to stop talking. He gave me a wink and jogged back to the riders who were busily organizing themselves into mixed teams for some of our, well, their, favourite games.

I sighed and walked towards the cross-country course, every step bringing back memories of riding it. From the ground the jumps looked huge. I swallowed hard, wondering if I would ever be able to take on the fences again. My hands started shaking as I scribbled the words 'too big' on the first fresh page of the notepad. I felt tired and breathless all of a sudden and sat on a log under some trees. I breathed in through my nose and out through my mouth, but it was no use. The tingles were washing over me like waves, huge relentless waves that I could no longer control. I closed my eyes and squeezed the notepad tight, then shoved it into my pocket and shook my hands as hard as I could.

'Hey, Spills,' said a voice.

I blew out a long breath and opened my eyes. The sunlight seemed stronger than usual and made me squint. 'Nick off, Carly.'

Carly said something else to me that ended in 'off'. She sat on Destiny's back, watching me, her feet dangling from her stirrups in their scuffed black boots, waiting for me to do something, anything.

'Heard you had a bad dream,' she said, her eyes burning. 'Oh, poor baby.'

I was beginning to feel sick. My heart started to thump hard.

'Flea reckons he can hear you from his place, crying for your mum. And your dad's telling anyone who'll listen about your big sob story. You are such a loser.'

'Haven't you found anyone new to harass at high

school?' I said. My voice was shrill but I tried to sigh like I was bored.

'Nobody as pathetic as you.' Carly laughed. I looked over her shoulder. Flea and Ryan were still whooping around the club grounds, oblivious that she'd ridden off. That was the thing about Carly. The thing that made her different from so many of the other bullies I'd ever known. She could do it alone. She didn't need anyone standing beside her or behind her to make her feel tough enough to be mean. It was just her.

I stood up and looked at Carly, right into her eyes.

'You need help,' I said. I started to head back towards the office. That was something I'd tried to teach myself since the accident. I didn't have to be a hero. It was okay to walk away sometimes.

'You're the one that needs help!' Carly snapped.

I paused, remembering holding her hand as we sat by Destiny waiting for the vet. I'd been there for her when she'd needed me. Becky had stood up for her, gotten help for the sweet mare who'd nearly lost her life thanks to Carly's selfishness and stupidity. 'On second thoughts, maybe what you need is more attention from your parents. I'm sure they love you deep down. Deep, deep, deep down.'

Carly's face darkened. I knew I'd hit a raw nerve and felt very mean. But she deserved it, I told myself.

I heard her cough and realized she was crying and felt meaner than mean. It was people like her and India McCray — the girl from Linley Heights who'd dared me to ride Lightning in the first place — people like them who said terrible things. Not people like me.

I took a step towards her.

'I'm sorry!' I said. 'I didn't mean it.' I reached out and touched her knee. 'I'm really sorr—'

Carly rammed her feet into her stirrups and pulled up hard on her reins. Her face was red and streaked with tears. Destiny threw her head high and I ducked, terrified, and fell hard on my knees.

'You loser!' Carly shrieked. 'You big loser!'

I scrambled to my feet and ran towards the office, stumbling over sticks and my own joggers. Adrenalin pumped through my body. Run, my brain ordered, run, run, run! Carly chased after me. The mare was close behind me. I could almost feel her confusion. Her whole life, all her training and her sweet nature had never prepared her for this, for cantering after a person.

I ran as fast as I could, looked over my shoulder, then tripped, fell again and lay sprawled on my back. Destiny bore down on me and I screamed, covering my face with my arms. I rolled over onto my hands and knees, dug my fingers into the dirt and screamed again then cried out, terrified. This was like the daymare — except it was real, like everything I'd ever feared, every nightmare I'd ever had was coming true. I was overcome by a strange, horrible feeling. Like I was sinking underwater, so far down that I couldn't breathe. My whole body shook. I curled up into a tight ball. My eyes squeezed shut and I waited for the shod hooves to crush my back and for the pain to come.

'Carly, back off!' called a voice. I started to cry.

Someone pulled on my arm but I resisted, turning my face away. Whoever they were I wanted them, Carly and the whole Riding Club to drop dead. I cried harder, sobbed, knowing that it was hopeless. It wasn't Carly who'd scared me. It was Destiny.

'Ashleigh, it's okay.' The owner of the voice pulled at my arm again. 'She's gone.'

I opened my eyes a little, taking huge gulps of air, and wiped my face with the back of my hand.

Flea was looking down at me with an expression I'd never seen on his face before. I realized for the first time that his eyes were blue. I'd never been close enough to notice before. I'd never cared.

'It's okay,' he said again, and offered me his hand. I looked at it for a moment. It was grubby, as usual, and his fingernails were filthy with horse grime. Just this morning I would never have considered taking his hand, expecting at the very least an electric shock or some kind of kung fu manoeuvre that would have me spinning through the air like a catherine-wheel to be unleashed upon me. But somehow I trusted him. I accepted his hand and he hauled me to my feet.

'Keep outta trouble,' he said, and he walked away. I noticed that Ryan was holding Scud's reins close by. 'And keep outta Carly's radar.'

I stood there for a moment, stunned, the last of my sobs slowly melting away, like they do when things really dawn on you for the first time. Riding Club had always been a place where I'd learned something new about horses. A place where I could be myself. That morning I'd learned about people. I'd learned that Carly could be hurt in the same way she hurt others. I'd learned that Flea could surprise me, not in the usual ways, but with kindness. And as I watched Gary, Becky and Pree running towards me, fear on their faces, I learned that I could never, no matter what, ever ride a horse again.

three

Grand Plans

'Some day, huh?'

'You can say that again.' I rested my head against Becky's. We were snuggled up together under my doona watching DVDs from Linley. Our polocrosse games were usually filmed so we could watch ourselves later and think of ways to improve our game. But right now all I could think was, 'Who's that girl on the grey horse?' Honey hadn't been ready for polocrosse so I had played on Mystery, a cute grey mare who was so experienced that she almost played the game for me.

'Some day, huh?' came a muffled voice from under the doona.

'Very funny, Pree,' I grumbled.

It had been an unbelievable day. Not unbelievable good, unbelievable surreal. Gary had wound Riding Club up early and brought me home, filling Mum and Dad in on all the details. Dad had given me a thorough once-over and declared that although I'd managed to add a few more bruises to my collection I wouldn't have to go back to hospital. But Mum had fussed over me like an old chook, kissing me all over my face and sending me straight to bed. I'd wailed and moaned and she'd sweetened the sentence by saying that Becky and Pree could stay for dinner and some DVDs, but I had to be in bed and resting by eight o'clock that night at the very ultimate latest.

'An oldie, but a baddie.' Becky reached into the huge bag of corn chips on the bedside table.

Pree sat up, tossing the doona around. 'An oldie, but a goldie. And speaking of goldies, how do you lead a horse to water?'

Becky and I looked at each other and rolled our eyes. 'How?' we chorused.

'With lots of carrots!' Pree collapsed in a fit of giggles. 'I crack myself up. Okay, how 'bout this one. What animal has more hands than feet? A horse! D'you get it? Horses are measured in hands!'

'I can do better than that. Check this out.' Becky shoved two corn chips under her top lip and growled like a tiger.

'Gross,' I said. I scooped up a crackerful of spicy cream-coloured dip and licked it up then stuck out my tongue and crossed my eyes.

'You win,' Becky said. She tapped my head and both my shoulders with a corn chip. 'I name thee Queen of Gross.'

I smiled and pushed dip through my teeth with my tongue. 'Fang goo.'

'That's disgusting,' Becky said. 'You know, Ash—'

I held up my hand. 'When addressing me, at all times use my official title.'

Pree giggled and stuffed a handful of corn chips into her mouth. 'You're bonkers.'

'You know, Queen of Gross,' Becky began again.

I bowed deeply and gave her the royal wave.

'We really need to get a polocrosse team happening at Riding Club. Doncha think that'd be an awesome idea?'

'Foogy ahhoom,' Pree said. Chunks of soggy chewed-up corn chip sprayed across my doona.

'What was that?' Becky cocked her head to one side and regarded Pree.

Pree swallowed and brushed corn chip chunks from the doona onto the floor. 'Fully awesome.'

'See?' Becky said. Her eyes were alight. 'It's a great idea, fantastic, the best!'

Pree clapped her hands and bounced on the bed. 'We're gonna have a polocrosse team, we're gonna have a polocrosse team!'

I held up my hands in the 'T' for time-out sign. 'Who's gonna coach you guys? Who's gonna get you the gear? Who's gonna get you a team to verse?'

'The Ridge'll verse 'em,' Pree said. She was so excited her hair was practically standing on end. 'It'll be sooo cool! We'll see each other every weekend and play and then afterwards we can go to Rebecca's Garden and—'

'Hey!' Becky said, prickly all of a sudden. We knew she hated that her parents had named their Chinese restaurant after her. Personally, I'd have been pretty stoked if mine had named their B and B 'Ashleigh Is the Most Incredible Daughter in the Whole Entire World Lodge', but they settled on boring old Miller Lodge (aka Spiller Splodge — no prizes for guessing who came up with that!).

'Relax,' I said, rubbing my tummy. I was hungry for chocolate ice cream. I was hungry for anything chocolate, actually. 'Who's gonna coach you?'

Becky looked at Pree. They smiled. I knew what was coming before they even opened their mouths.

'You!' they said together.

I folded my arms and shook my head, my eyes squeezed shut. 'No. Uh-uh. No way. Not a chance.'

'But why not?' my two best friends whined in unison.

I let my mouth fall open, shock-style. 'Did you guys see what happened today? Do you know what's going on with me or not? I can't ride anymore. I couldn't even get near a rocking horse. Not for all the maize in Melbourne.'

Becky and Pree exchanged a very worried glance. I knew why. This wasn't the Ash they knew. The Ash they knew would be saying 'yes', and making posters and raising money and belting around the Shady Creek Riding Club grounds with a number on her shirt and a stick in her hand.

But I wasn't the same person. Not since the accident. I was trying, but the nightmares were winning.

'If you really loved us, you'd coach us,' Pree said.

'Now I know why my oldies get annoyed when I say that,' I said, waggling my finger, irritated-parent-style. 'I do love you, both of you. But I don't have to prove it by doing something I can't do.'

'But why not?' they whined again.

'Number one, the doctors haven't said I can ride yet,' I said, ticking off on my fingers. 'Number two, I'm not ready. Number three, I'm, uh, I'm—'

'You're what?' Pree asked softly, her huge dark eyes searching mine.

'I—I—' I stammered. I wanted to tell her so badly. I wanted to tell both of them how scared I was. But, afraid as I was of riding horses again there was a bigger fear, one that was even more terrifying. What if they stopped liking me? What if not riding made me lose them? What if they grew closer together and left me behind? Who would I be if I wasn't a rider? What would my life be about? Horses had been my world for so long now I didn't know what I would do without them.

I took a deep breath. Becky and Pree watched me. 'I think you'd better go now. I'm so tired.'

'But it's only six-thirty,' Becky said.

I shook my head. 'I need to rest.'

Becky and Pree exchanged a glance and shrugged, but did as I asked. I wished them goodnight and a good day at school, asked them to turn off the light and lay down flat in my bed, pulling my doona up under my chin. Once the voices downstairs had stopped and I heard the front door click I knew they were gone. I sat up in bed and opened the drawer of my bedside table, pulling out my mobile phone. I had to talk to someone. I had to get some answers and the best person in the whole world to find them was the one person who knew me best.

I texted as fast as I could and hit the send button, sighing with relief as a little envelope flew across the tiny screen. This was an emergency. I needed Jenna online and I needed her now.

'Earth to Ashleigh, come in, Ashleigh.' I looked at my mother. She was looking back at me, one eyebrow raised, both hands on the steering wheel. We'd been driving for nearly three hours and I felt sick inside and in no mood for chitchat. 'Are your ears switched on? I asked you three times already. Why do you wanna go back to school so soon? Why did it have to be today?'

I shrugged. 'Just had to be. Had to go back. Don't wanna get too far behind in my studies.'

'Hmm.' Mum had this look on her face, like she thought there was something fishy going on. 'Since when are you worried about getting behind in your studies?'

'Horsiness works in mysterious ways,' I grouched, glaring out of the window so that she knew that I didn't want to talk about it anymore. The drive to Linley Heights School wasn't exactly exciting. Trees, scrub, grey-green rocks that seemed to grow out of the ground, and more scrub.

'Thank goodness Jason's on the bottle now. Gives me a chance to spend some time with my best girl.' She was trying hard to sound upbeat.

'I'm your only girl.'

'Thank goodness.' Mum reached over to tousle my hair.

I gave her the 'stop' sign. 'I thought we agreed I was way too old for that.'

'You agreed.' Mum fidgeted with the rear-view mirror. 'As far as I'm concerned you're never too old. I seem to remember you sneaking into bed with your dad and me a few nights ago.'

'If you ever tell that to anyone, I'll get a nose ring.' I flipped down the sunvisor and examined my face in the mirror. A freckle-faced girl with dark hair and eyes looked back at me. I gave her a grin and checked my teeth for bits. 'Can Dad be trusted with Jason?'

'As long as he doesn't take him to the pub.'

'Did he take me to the pub when I was a baby?' I tucked my hair behind my ears and pulled my world-famous monkey face at myself.

'Only on chook raffle night.' Mum laughed at her own dumb joke. 'Hey, I think we're getting close.'

'Great.' I sighed. The tingles kicked in. I was getting used to them, but that didn't mean I liked them.

'I still say you could've started back next week, possum. I can't understand you worrying about getting behind when the school sent you enough work to keep you going for a year and the doctors told you to rest. I just don't understand the rush.'

I flipped the visor back up and crossed my arms. 'Have you forgotten what happened to me at Riding Club?'

'Now we're getting somewhere.' Mum scowled. 'You can't run away from your problems, Ash.'

'Sure I can. I'm doing it now.'

'Running away doesn't solve anything.'

'Says who?'

'Gary barred Carly for a month and her parents have grounded her from riding Destiny for a week. Doesn't that make you feel better?'

I gave her a look. What was it about grown-ups? What happened to them after they had their own kids that made them forget what it was like to be one? I was so glad I'd chatted to Jenna online. My best friend from the city had been right. One hundred per cent, exactamundo right. Bullies usually got worse when you dobbed them in. If I stayed in Shady Creek any longer I'd wind up with more than just a few bruises to show for it. I had an out and I wasn't afraid of taking it. 'Why would I feel better?'

'Are you sure you didn't do anything to upset Carly?' Mum asked, one eyebrow raised.

I gaped at her, pushing the memory of the mean things I'd said to Carly out of my mind. Well, to the side of it anyway. 'I told you, no.'

'In that case she got what she deserved.' Mum tucked a wisp of my hair behind my ear.

'Honestly!' I groaned and slapped my forehead with my palms, more frustrated with my possible compulsive lying affliction than with her. 'Don't you people understand? She's gonna want to get me even more now.'

'Don't be silly. And don't call me "you people". You teenagers can be so … what am I saying? You're only twelve. Ooh, there it is!' Mum put on her right blinker as the sandstone turrets came into view. My tummy spun.

I felt like I'd been away for years, but Linley Heights School was the same as I remembered it. The main school building that looked like a castle was still there. The huge lawn, flowerbeds and playing fields were strikingly green compared to the sparse, dry, yellow and brown paddocks we'd driven past on the way. The wooden double doors were closed, making the place look even more like something from the Middle Ages. All it needed was a moat. I shuddered, thinking about the many nasty creatures in Linley uniforms that could easily take the place of crocodiles in any medieval moat, and wondered if perhaps I'd been a little hasty in wanting to come back early.

Mum parked the car and switched off the engine, but neither of us moved.

'You ready?' Mum rested her hand on my knee.

I shook my head. 'Not sure. I feel a bit … a bit funny.'

'Funny ha-ha or funny awful?' Mum gave my knee a squeeze. I knew she was trying. I looked at her hand and noticed for the first time that her hands and mine were so much alike. Same freckles, same fingers, same short nails.

'I don't know if I belong here, Mum. Or in Shady Creek. If I can't ride anymore what's going to happen to me?' There. I'd finally said it.

'If you don't want to ride again, that's up to you, poss.' Mum took my hand in hers. 'Your dad and I will never force you to ride or not ride. And we'd never make you give up Honey even if you never sat on her back again. We'd worry a whole lot less if you didn't ride, that's for sure.' She sighed and kissed the back of my hand. 'But the only thing that really terrifies us both is you not being you, because when you can't be yourself, you can only ever be miserable.'

My eyes filled with tears and I took a long shaky breath. Maybe she was right. Maybe that's why I'd been feeling so rotten. Maybe it wasn't the riding after all. Maybe, just maybe, it was the not riding that was making me feel this way. Maybe the one and only thing that would put an end to the nightmares once and for all was getting back into the saddle.

Mum had carried my bags to my room, kissed and hugged me then left. I was alone. I sat on my bed for a while looking around the room. My half was pretty much the same as I had left it. My horse posters and photos were tacked to the wall, my doona was smooth, my desk was scattered with school and horse books and my pencil case was open with its contents spilling out. Someone had emptied my clothes hamper and, when I checked my closet, I found that my uniform had been washed and was hanging up, ready for Term Two.

I stared at Claire's side of the room, sterile as ever, and thought about how stoked she must have been having our room all to herself and how disappointed she'd be that I'd come back early. Then I thought that it was probably time for me to visit Mrs Freeman. There were lots of things I had to tell her.

The principal was usually too busy to see anyone straightaway but she made a special exception for me. I was ushered into her office by her secretary and sat as still and quiet as I could in the stiff red leather chair opposite hers. Her office was huge, more like an apartment, and decorated with photos, trophies, framed pieces of paper with red stamps on them and rows and rows of books. Mrs Freeman sat at her desk, dressed immaculately as usual in a neat grey suit. Her golden, chin-length hair was perfect and smooth. I cleared my throat and stared hard at my lap, waiting for the lecture to begin.

'It's good to see you've come back to us, Ashleigh. You gave me quite a fright, you know.'

I looked up at once, surprised, then hung my head, too ashamed to look into her kind eyes.

'You gave all of us a fright.'

I braced myself, knowing it was coming.

'I've spent a great deal of time thinking about what I should do with you.'

'Am I going to be expelled?' I gasped.

Mrs Freeman shook her head.

'Suspended?'

'No.'

'I'm sorry! I'm sorry for the whole thing. I'm sorry for Demi and the other riders. Please don't let the horse haters win! I heard about the inquiry and the meeting and I'm so scared.' I knew I was babbling. There was so much inside my head but not enough room to fit it all in my mouth. 'Please tell them it was my fault! Please tell them the riding program and Lightning aren't to blame!'

Mrs Freeman sighed. 'I appreciate what you said. And I appreciate that you're accepting responsibility. That shows a great deal of maturity and I'm proud of you for that.'

I lit up inside. I wanted her to be proud of me.

'But I'm going to be asking you to write Demi and the School Board a letter of apology and an assurance that nothing like that will ever happen again. Linley Heights expects a great deal from its girls, scholarship girls in particular.'

I nodded. A letter of apology. I could handle that. 'And I wanted to thank you.'

'For?'

I took a breath. 'For staying with me. For going in the ambulance with me.'

Mrs Freeman smiled gently. 'You're very welcome. Let's just make sure that we never have to make another trip like it.'

I smiled back. 'Okay.'

'Have you managed to get to the riding centre yet? I think there's a horse down there that's been missing her mistress.'

'I'd like to go,' I said hesitantly. 'But shouldn't I get to class?'

Mrs Freeman shook her head. 'Not today. Take some time to settle back in.'

I thanked her again and left.

It had been weeks since I'd seen Honey. The last time I'd touched her, smelled her horsy smell and told her I loved her was the day of the accident. It seemed like so much longer. I wondered if she'd even remember me.

I had assured Mrs Freeman that I was okay to go to the stables myself. I knew it was something I had to do. I tried to summon up every ounce of bravery I had. I was sure I had a stockpile of it somewhere inside. Yesterday at Riding Club there'd been a whole lot of fear. Every time I had the nightmare there was a whole lot of panic. Thinking about Honey and how I would feel if she rejected me, there was a whole lot of pain.

I walked down the path to the stables. Honey would be in her paddock, the mares' paddock. I hoped she was safe, that she'd be free of kicks, bites and lumps. I hoped that she'd found her place in the herd, that the other mares had accepted her into their community. I hoped that she'd found a friend. I knew that horses always hooked up with a friend and that friends in the paddock were as important to horses as friends in the playground were to us humans. Honey had had Toffee and I'd hated separating them when I came to Linley.

The tack room was wall-to-wall saddles, bridles, helmets, halters and lead ropes. There were lunging lines on hooks and whips in barrels. There were polocrosse sticks and rugs and boxes and travel bandages. I walked around the room slowly, running my fingers over the tack, memories of horsy times and places flooding my head at every touch.

My gear had been put back after the challenge. Someone had untacked Honey's saddle and bridle from Lightning, cleaned it up and put it neatly away. I sighed, relieved. My room at home and my desk at school might have been chaotic, but I always took care of my tack. Honey's saddle blanket rested upside down on top of her saddle. By the looks of it, it had been washed. The good fairies of Linley had done something nice for me while I was gone.

'Hello, young missy,' a voice behind me said. It was Joe. He was one of the best horse handlers in the known universe and had taught me to think from Honey's point of view about her move from Shady Creek to Linley.

'Hi, Joe.' I took my bridle down from its hook and held it, rubbing my fingers into the soft, sweet-smelling leather.

'Haven't seen you for a little while.' Joe's freckled face crinkled into a grin. 'Been up to no good?'

I smiled dryly. 'Something like that.'

Joe patted my head. I knew he was trying to tell me that he understood. 'Your filly's fine, Missy. Just fine. Been eatin' well, settled right down in the paddock. Even made a friend. That pony, Rose. Another chestnut. Two of 'em have been inseparable.'

I smiled, relief washing over me. My Honey horse was okay.

'I s'pose you wanna catch up with that filly of yours?'

I nodded.

'Feel okay about going into the paddock alone?' Joe looked at me, his dark eyes serious.

I shook my head.

'Want me to come along? Help out a bit?'

I nodded, feeling breathless. 'Yes!'

I replaced the bridle and took Honey's thick red cotton lead rope and pink-and-purple synthetic halter from their hooks and held onto them tightly. Joe and I walked towards the paddock together. Every step was taking me closer to Honey. Every step was another on my journey. Every step, I hoped, was taking me closer to recovering.

Joe unlatched the gate to the mares' paddock. 'After you.'

I took a step inside, my heart pumping. I could see the mares gathered in the far right-hand corner of the paddock. Two chestnut horses were grazing side by side. Another group, about six or so, were gathered around the huge bay mare with the fly eyes.

I slapped my forehead. 'I forgot treats! I never catch Honey without a slice of carrot.'

Joe patted the pocket of his horse-grubby shorts. 'No worries, Missy. Call out to her.'

'Honey!' I called. 'Honey!'

A chestnut mare raised her head and looked up at me, then dropped it again and continued grazing. I knew what she was thinking. *You ride some other horse behind my back, leave me here alone for weeks then show up without a carrot and expect me to come running?*

'Honey!' I called again. 'Hoonnnneyyy!'

The mare raised her head again and whinnied, taking her first step towards me. My heart leapt.

'Wave this at your filly,' Joe said, pushing a slice of carrot into my hand.

I held the carrot above my head. 'Hoonnnneyyy!'

My Honey horse whinnied again and her friend joined her. The two horses walked together up the slight hill towards Joe and me. To my horror, Fly Eyes and her posse of ponies followed them. Joe had given me enough carrot for one horse. The thought of being surrounded by a pack of mares all after the same strip of tasty titbit made me sweat. In my old life I'd have pushed their chests and shown them who was boss. But my old life seemed lost forever.

Honey was on her way. Her ears were pricked forward. She whinnied again and broke into a trot. Her friend, Rose, a similar-looking chestnut with a white star on her sweet face and four white socks, followed closely behind. Fly Eyes bore down on them, anxious not to miss out on a treat.

Honey got closer. I walked towards her. Joe stayed close knowing I couldn't do it alone.

'Remember,' Joe said. 'Diagonally, Missy. Never walk at a horse in a straight line when you're trying to catch 'em.'

I zigzagged towards Honey, just a little way, looking over my shoulder to make sure that Joe was still there.

It wasn't long before she was standing in front of me. I held my hand out flat, the titbit balanced on my palm. She nuzzled my palm and accepted the slice of carrot, chewing it slowly, then searched my hand for another. Her whiskers tickled my hand and I giggled, then looped the lead rope around her neck and held both ends with my right hand. I shook out her halter with my left hand and placed the noseband over her nose, clipping the lead rope to the ring under her chin. I kept a hold of the lead rope with my right hand and pulled the headpiece around her head, behind her ears, then buckled it up at her cheek. I pulled her forelock out from underneath her browband, then leaned forward and kissed her nose. I wrapped my arms around her neck and held her close for a while, watching Joe shooing away the other mares, then, taking her lead rope in my right hand and holding up the slack with my left, I led my gorgeous chestnut mare from her paddock.

four

My Fair Pony

'How've you been?' I rubbed my cheek against Honey's and held her head in my hands. Joe had disappeared and there was nobody else in the stalls. I loved the Linley stalls. Every horse had their own. They were cool in summer and I'd been told (and hoped!) they were snug in winter. It was a wonderful, horsy place to be. It was so good to be alone with my Honey horse. 'I missed you so much.'

I took a step back and looked at her. It was like seeing her for the first time. My heart felt so heavy with love for her. She was so many things to me. She was a true and loyal friend. She worked so hard to please me and had always tried to learn new things. I'd ridden her in cross-country, dressage, Riding

Club games, gymkhanas and shows and she'd never let me down. She'd even saved me and Charlie, Becky's gorgeous bay gelding, from the bushfire that had ripped through Shady Creek the year before. I owed her so much.

'I'm going to give you a good groom,' I told her, unclipping her light cotton rug. The days were still warm and mild, so the rug was there as a sort of sunhat rather than for warmth. It also gave her a bit of protection from the politics of the paddock. Since moving to Linley, Honey had had her fair share of nips, kicks and bites. I folded the rug over her rump, then over again and, running my hand along her rump and far side, I unclipped the front clips and folded back the front half of the rug. I scooped it up under my right arm and dragged it off her back then spread it out, upside down, on the wall of the stall to air. I ran my hands down Honey's body, from her neck, over her withers and down her back. Her coat was warm under my hands. Her sensitive muscles twitched. I held her for a while, feeling her body move as she breathed, and thought about everything that had happened over the past six weeks. Words and pictures tumbled around in my mind. Some of them weren't very nice. I tilted my head and banged on my ear, hoping that all the bad thoughts would ooze out, like water after swimming. I decided that getting on with the groom was the best thing to do for Honey and for me.

It was time to clean Honey's feet.

I rummaged in my grooming kit for my favourite hoof pick and tucked it into the back pocket of my jeans, then rested my left hand on Honey's near shoulder and ran my right hand down her near foreleg, feeling carefully for any lumps, swelling or heat, all of which could mean an injury. The last thing I wanted was for Honey to have an injured leg. 'Up,' I said, once I had a firm hold of her pastern, and Honey lifted her foot willingly. I raised it to the height of my shin and wedged her foot between my knees, then held her foot with my left hand and pulled the hoof pick from my pocket with my right.

I was glad to see that her foot was mostly clear. Joe had been caring for her really well. I removed some mud and poo with the hoof pick, moving the pick from her heel to her toe (being very aware of her frog, the sensitive triangle-shaped pad in the centre of her foot) and noticed that a small stone was lodged in the mud. Once her hoof was clear I pressed gently on the sole of her foot, checking for any tenderness, then made sure that her shoe was secure. She looked about due for a shoeing and I made a mental note to book her in with Joe, who did all the shoeing of the Linley school horses and many of the boarders' horses as well. Some girls preferred to use their own farriers, but I trusted Joe completely with Honey's feet.

I set her foot down gently then approached her near hind foot. Picking up hind feet is a bit different and can be tricky. I rested my hand on Honey's hip joint to let her know what I was about to do and that she'd soon have to shift her weight to her other foot. I patted her gaskin, her hind thigh, and moved my hand down her leg, over her hock and to her fetlock.

'Up!' I said, pushing gently against her hip. I lifted her foot up and a little forward and, taking a step closer to her body with my left foot, wedged her foot between my knees. I cleaned her foot and set it down, then moved on to her other feet.

I loved grooming Honey, spending time with her like this. It was just her and me, no distractions, no pressure.

I chose a rubber currycomb from my grooming kit and gently removed the caked mud from each of her legs. I ran a dandy-brush across her back in the direction her hair grew, flicking the brush up at the end of each stroke to lift the dirt, then groomed her whole body with a body brush. Once she was shining I wiped her with a damp cloth and got to work on her mane, spraying it with detangler, untangling it with my fingers then brushing it gently with the dandy-brush. I did the same thing all over again on her tail then stood back to admire the new and improved Honey.

'Looking good!' a voice behind me called.

I grabbed my chest, spooked, and spun around. It was just like Riding Club — my pumping heart flooded my arms and legs with adrenalin.

'Emily!' I scrambled out of the stall door and threw my arms around my friend's neck. I was instantly wrapped in another pair of arms and long, dark curls. 'Ricki the Remarkable!'

Emily Phuong stepped back and beamed at me, her eyes shining from behind her round glasses. It was Term Two and winter uniform was upon us all, even though it was still warm. Em's long, light blue sleeves were rolled up to her armpits and her striped, navy and white tie was loose. She'd let her long winter socks pool around her ankles and the belt that was supposed to be tight around her waist was floating. 'We heard you were back.'

'And we came straightaway.' Ricki Samuels's face was glowing. I hoped it was from the joy of our reunion and not just from the thick fabric she was swathed in. She pulled her magic wand from her pinafore pocket and held it reverently in both hands. 'Transported to this very stall by the power of the magic that is contained within this humble wand.'

'By the power of the magic that's contained within our feet, more like,' Emily said, rolling her eyes. 'So, how you going, Ash?'

I shook my head, annoyed by my still-aching legs. I never used to startle like this before and I didn't understand it any more than I liked it.

I told them about Shady Creek and Riding Club and about my nightmares. I told them about Carly and my back and my neck. I told them about my fears. They nodded and glanced at each other every now and then and then back at me, their eyes filled with concern. They knew me as horse mad and proud. Ashleigh Miller without horses and riding in her life would be like Ricki without magic, or Em without Maths, or a History class without Mrs Wright giving out lunch detentions.

'I think I know what you need,' Ricki said, smiling.

I shrugged. 'What?'

Emily and Ricki smiled at each other and then at me. 'Lunch!' they said together.

My stomach, reminded at last that it hadn't eaten since breakfast in Shady Creek, growled in protest. 'We'd better get to the dorm. What's the time? Have we missed the food? What am I gonna do with Honey?'

Emily made a 'this way' gesture and I patted Honey, told her I'd be back soon and made sure she had clean fresh water and a full haynet, then followed Em out of the stalls. Just outside, under a tree and overlooking the paddocks and the back of the school, was a picnic rug and on that rug there was a basket.

'What's going on here?' I said, looking from one friend to the other, a huge smile on my face. It was the first time I felt like I'd really smiled in days.

'I'll tell you what's going on here,' Ricki said. She sat on the blanket, opened up the basket and pulled out plates, forks, cups, napkins and a large plastic tub. She opened the lid and delicious smells came out. 'My mum's voraciously very veritable Vietnamese noodles!'

I sat beside Ricki on the rug, my mouth watering as she served me up a huge pile of soft, flat white noodles. They were tossed with what looked like strips of beef and red and green veggies so crisp and tasty-looking that vitamins were practically bursting out of them. Emily poured us each a cup of sweet orange soft drink and we clinked plastic disposables.

'To us,' Ricki said.

'To Ash coming back at last.' Emily stuck out her foot and nudged mine.

'To lunch,' I said.

We drank to it.

Two serves of the most delicious noodle meal I'd ever eaten, a cup and a half of fizzy and most of a chocolate donut later, I lay flat on my back and rubbed at my tummy. 'That was in-cred-i-ble!' I said, stressing every syllable. 'I can't believe your mum can cook like this, Rick.'

Ricki dabbed at her dark eyes, mock-crying. 'She can't. We stopped for takeaway on the way to school this morning.'

'How'd you get it so hot?' I was doing calculations in my head.

Ricki stopped dabbing immediately and fluttered

her eyelashes. 'Charm will get you everywhere, Ash, my friend.'

'Speaking of charm, there's something we think you should know. About India and what she's done.' Emily's eyes were suddenly serious.

My tummy flip-flopped but I rolled my eyes and tried to sound like India McCray was the least of my worries. 'Apart from nearly having me killed, I simply can't imagine.'

Em and Ricki looked at each other. I knew straightaway that they had something bad to tell me.

'You heard about how one of those girls filmed you on her mobile, right?' Emily cleared her throat, like whatever she wanted to say was stuck.

I nodded.

'Well,' Em said. 'She, that girl, was India, and before she got her phone taken, she put you on the Internet.'

'So?' I said. I'd been on the Internet before. Holly from South Beach Stables had had a website and she'd always posted our show results. I sat up and popped the last chunk of my donut into my mouth, brushed my hands together then swallowed. Why did things that were so bad for you have to taste so good? 'Yummy.'

Ricki sighed. 'Ash, you don't understand. India put you on the Internet to make fun of you. She ran this horrible music over the footage and called you a bad name.'

I was shocked. My mouth fell open and I felt sick. The noodles I'd eaten turned over in my stomach and I was sure for a moment that everything inside me was going to come up.

'Are you okay?' Em grabbed my hand and squeezed my fingers, nudging at Ricki's foot.

I nodded. My mouth was dry. 'What bad name did she call me?'

Em shook her head. 'What does it matter now? It's been taken off.'

'No,' I snapped. 'You have to tell me. You can't tell me this much then decide when to stop. That's not fair. It wasn't you on that horse, was it? It wasn't you in hospital and it wasn't you on the Internet. So tell me!'

Tears welled in Em's eyes. I'd hurt her. I knew what she was trying to do. She wanted to protect me. Why did I do this so often? Why did I always open my mouth before I thought things through?

It was my turn to squeeze Em's hand. 'I'm sorry. I shouldn't have taken it out on you. I'm sorry.'

Em smiled weakly. 'We know it sucks, Ash. We know you need to know. We thought you'd find out at home but—'

I was on my feet in an instant. 'My parents know? They know and they didn't tell me?'

'That's how they saw the accident, Ash. The school got it off pretty fast, but they kept a copy. They had to. Do you think the kid just handed her phone over to your mum?' Ricki said simply.

'So what did she call me?' I decided at that moment that I wasn't going to be a victim anymore.

Ricki grimaced. 'She called you a bucking bronco—'

Emily cut in, red-faced. 'Something else starting with "B".'

'Welcome to Linley Heights,' I muttered. 'I thought this was s'posed to be a good school. What are people paying all this money for when stuff like this happens?'

Ricki laughed. 'You're not paying, Miss Scholarship.'

'That's not the point,' I grouched. 'Did she get kicked out? I heard she got suspended but what other trouble did she get in?'

Emily shook her head. 'That's it. Suspended.'

I pulled at my hair. 'That's it? That's unbelievable! Why should I have to go to school with a creep like that?'

'I'll fix 'er up, Ash,' Ricki said solemnly. 'I'll *ookakabooka* India into the next dimension. Just you wait, Ash, my old friend. I've been practising all holidays. I'm getting really good.'

'It's true,' said Em. 'She *ookakabooka*'d her sister to Coober Pedy last weekend. There's still no trace of her.'

'But I heard she's making a killing in opals.' Ricki giggled. There was a dusting of gold sparkles in her hair.

'It's time to get serious,' I said. Determination flooded through my body. I liked how it felt. I usually only felt like this when I was at a show or in a polocrosse game or twisting my horse around a barrel racing course. 'We're not gonna take this anymore!'

Ricki scrambled to her feet and dug around in her pinafore pocket for a handful of glitter. 'I'm with you.'

Em joined us. 'Me too!'

Ricki laughed and threw the glitter over our heads. 'That's it, guys. We just made a magical pact. It's unbreakable.'

'What did we pact to?' Em's eyes were wide.

'To not being pushed around by the Indias of the world!' I cried.

'Or the Indias of Linley,' Ricki chorused.

'And to being horse mad forever.' I wrapped an arm around each of my friends.

'Horse mad forever!' we sang together.

five

The Girl Can't Help It

I looked at myself in the mirror. A serious, dark-haired girl in the Linley Heights School winter uniform looked back at me. She wore a dark navy pinafore over a long-sleeved light blue shirt, a striped navy and white tie, long dark navy socks and shiny black shoes. There was a dark navy panama hat on her head, complete with ribbon and school crest, and a dark navy jumper slung over her arm. Her hair was tied in a conservative ponytail at the base of her neck. She shuddered.

'Wow,' I said. 'Wow and wow.'

I just couldn't believe the girl in the mirror was me. And I wasn't the only one.

'It was so good here without you.' My loving

roommate, Claire Carlson, stood behind me and scowled. Her dark bushy hair was pulled into a tight bun, making her eyes look even rounder than usual. 'I was the only girl in Year Seven to have a private room. I'm sure you'll be pleased to know that I disinfected your side of the room while you were away.'

'I'm thrilled,' I said, tucking a stray wisp of hair behind my ear. 'Who wouldn't be?'

'You were talking in your sleep last night, you know.'

I whipped around and looked at Claire. Her face was curled tightly in a smug smile. 'What did I say?'

'That's for me to know and for you to find out.'

My fists curled up and my chest swelled with anger. I'd been so stressed about going back to classes that it had taken me ages to fall asleep. I'd just lain in bed, feeling panic washing over me again and again like waves, until I'd felt sick. Claire's snoring and the silence of the rest of the dorm had made me feel even more mad that I was still awake and for a moment I'd wished I'd never come back to Linley.

When I'd finally fallen asleep I'd had another nightmare. I'd woken up in the dark, crying out, sweating. Why couldn't they have given me my own room for a while? Just until the bad dreams went away?

I hated Claire and everything she stood for. After all, it was Claire and her mother who'd been trying so hard to close the riding program at Linley. The accident could only help their cause. It made me sick to think that I, the person who'd fought so hard against them, had given them their greatest weapon. I didn't want to ride anymore. I couldn't. But I didn't want the horses to go. I didn't want the other horse tragics to suffer.

Claire settled her panama hat on her head. 'Going down for breakfast?'

I rolled my eyes and grabbed my schoolbag. It was crammed full of all the books I needed for the day, plus my diary, pencil cases and my music folder. I snatched at my violin case with my empty hand. 'What d'you care?'

'Actually, I don't,' Claire said.

'Good,' I spat, and left the room. I was the new tough Ashleigh. The don't-mess-with-me Ashleigh. The you'd-better-watch-out Ashleigh. But inside I was terrified. It was my first day back in class. My first day of bells and timetables and homework and

Mrs Wright. And it was the first time I'd see India since the accident.

I met Em in the dining room. She sat opposite me, tucking in to a huge plate of eggs, sausages and toast. I watched her, feeling more nauseated with every bite she took.

'You'd better make the most of this, Ash. Tomorrow we'll be back to stale cereal and powdered milk.' Em stabbed at the mountain of scrambled egg on her plate with her fork. 'I think this is real egg. Try it. It's really good.' She held out her fork and tried to force-feed me. 'Here comes the plane!'

'What is it with you and eggs?' I shook my head and drew back imagining Emily with sticky yellow goo dribbling down her hair. 'I can't.'

Em ate the egg then sliced off a chunk of sausage and waved it under my nose. 'You're crackers.'

'And all you ever think about is food.'

'Pretty much,' she said, pushing her glasses up on her nose. 'Have to in a place like this. You never know when your next decent meal might be. At least have a piece of toast. You can't face Mrs Wright on an empty stomach.'

'There's nothing empty about it. Full of dragonflies.' I grabbed at my aching tummy. 'Fire-breathing ones, I reckon.' Normally I would have eaten if there'd been anything crunchy on offer. Crunching on carrots or celery or corn chips always makes me feel better when I'm stressed. But sausages and scrambled eggs don't crunch. And I was starting to feel very sick. 'Em, I think I need to — I think I should—'

'Stuffing your face again? That'd be right.'

Em glanced up briefly then refocussed on her breakfast. 'Good morning, Mercedes. And what a joy it is to see your sunny face at this early hour.'

Mercedes Phuong, Em's big sister and total pain in the saddle sores extraordinaire, regarded us through cold, narrow eyes. Her one pleasure in life was catching Em doing the complete opposite of what she'd been told to do by her mum and promptly letting her know. Em had been frightened into staying well clear of Mercedes (or Murk as she was unaffectionately known to us) at school by the promise of having her eyebrows shaved off in her sleep.

Mercedes smiled. Well, she showed her teeth at us through tight, thin lips. 'Eat up, Emily. This could be your last meal.'

Murk stalked away, her black hair swishing, and Em stuck her finger in her mouth, vomit-style. 'Creep.'

'You said it.' I strained for a glimpse of India. Part of me wanted to stick her mobile phone up her nose, but there was another part that was sick with nerves at the thought of seeing her. The dining-room tables were packed with girls eating, texting or talking. Some were doing all three at once. Others were frantically finishing off homework. A few who had finished their breakfast had wads of brightly coloured gum wedged in their jaws. The whole room clanged with girly voices, forks on plates and metal serving spoons on hot, steaming trays. It smelled of breakfast and body spray.

Em scratched her head. 'What were you saying before? What do you need?'

I rubbed at my forehead. 'It's nothing, I ... I might need to ... don't worry about it.'

My head spun. I needed to talk to someone. I needed to be told what it was that was wrong with me.

'Whatcha got first?'

'Um, Maths. Then instrumental for a whole hour.' I glared at my violin case. My violin and I had a loathe-loathe relationship. I was going to return it to the planet it had come from and switch to another instrument. If I could convince Mrs Craig, the Head of Music, that I would be the best thing to happen to the bassoon since sliced carrots, that is.

Em pulled her diary from her bag and studied her timetable. 'When've you got Horsemanship? I can't wait to start.'

'Last period.' My tummy did more than just a flip-flop. It executed a perfect pike with a triple twist. My Horsemanship teacher was Demi James. My riding coach was Demi James. Lightning's owner was Demi James. 'When're you starting?'

'Next term, I hope. I just have to blitz Maths.' Em's parents were now okay with her becoming a vet instead of a doctor or lawyer as they would have liked, but she still couldn't start riding classes until she aced Maths.

'That's a given.' I sighed. Maths was a language I just didn't understand, lots of mere mortals didn't understand. And then there were the Emilys among us, those chosen few who not only understood it, but loved it. In moments of mathematically induced euphoria I'd actually heard her say, 'Maths is beautiful.'

We picked up our bags and headed off together towards the door. Assembly would start in a few minutes and we didn't want to be late. Just as we were walking through the dining-room door, India appeared, almost out of nowhere. Her eyes flashed and her face went red and she slammed her shoulder into mine as we passed.

'Hey!' I said. I'd promised myself I wasn't going to take it and there was no better time to start not taking it.

India kept walking, but cast a toxic look over her shoulder. I lurched after her, hungry to pinch or pull or scratch. Hungry to hurt her just like she'd hurt me.

'No!' Em cried, grabbing my arm. 'She's not worth it.'

I was breathing hard but I didn't resist, sense finally settling back down on my head. I'd been waiting for this moment for so long. I'd spent so much time thinking about what it would be like to see her face to face for the first time since the accident. I'd rehearsed the clever things I was going to say over and over in my head, and I'd fantasized about her begging for my forgiveness, apologizing to me in front of the whole school, sending me flowers, chocolates … anything. But, like so many moments in life, this one had turned out nothing like I'd hoped it would. I was starting to learn about people. You couldn't make them like you. You couldn't make them think the way you wanted them to. You couldn't change them. They had to do all those things for themselves.

'Besides,' Em said, taking me by the arms and looking into my eyes. 'You're better than that.'

I nodded and gulped. At that moment I knew I had to go and see someone. I'd have to talk. 'I'm not gonna let 'em do it anymore, Em. Not Carly, not India. None of 'em.'

Emily pulled me into a hug. 'Horse mad forever, okay?'

'Horse mad forever.'

'Welcome to Week Two.'

Demi James stood in front of the Horsemanship class. I looked straight at her, waiting for her eyes to settle on mine. I'd been dying for this lesson to start all day (especially after a violin lesson that had made fingernails scraping down a chalkboard sound like a siren's song). I was still in awe of her and couldn't help thinking how cool it was to have a teacher who wore joddies and boots. Demi was a top rider and the best riding teacher I'd ever had. She'd taught me in a way I'd never experienced before. The Linley girls said that she could have made it to the Olympics, but Lightning held her back. Most of them didn't get how anyone could throw an Olympic career down the trough for the love of a horse. But I did.

'Last week we began our new unit of inquiry into Horse Anatomy and Physiology, and for the benefit of my curiosity, and potentially my sanity, I'd like you to label the points of the horse on this sheet without opening anything but your brains. Let's see how much you have learned so far.' Demi passed worksheets around the class. Every girl was silent. She slapped a copy of the sheet down in front of me.

'Thank you, Miss,' I said.

'It's Demi,' Demi snapped.

I could hear India choking back laughter somewhere behind me and thanked the horse gods that Demi, unlike Mrs Wright (who I was sure had learned what she knew about medieval tortures in her former life as a dungeon guard), had never made us sit in alphabetical order.

I stared at my worksheet so hard the outline of the horse was still there when I closed my eyes. It seemed pretty basic to me. The horse had numbers sort of floating around it like butterflies. Arrows were pointing from the numbers to various parts of the horse's body. The same numbers were listed underneath the picture with blank lines beside them to write the answers. I scribbled down the answers quickly and pushed my sheet away.

'Finished already?' Demi was at my side in an instant.

I nodded.

'Have you filled in all the answers?'

I nodded again.

'Have you checked your work thoroughly?'

Before I had time to answer, Demi snatched up the sheet and pored over it. She looked down at me and smiled. 'Have a crack at the advanced sheet.'

'Advanced sheet?' I'd had no idea that points of the horse worksheets came in levels.

'Yep.' Demi strode to the teacher's desk and was back in a nanosecond with a new paper. I looked at it and gulped. There were fifty-three blank spaces to fill in and a second diagram of the hoof. I'd never tackled anything like it. On paper anyway. I gaped at Demi.

'Are you serious?'

Demi nodded sharply. 'You betcha bridle I am.'

A girl raised her hand and Demi was gone. I

82

rubbed at my forehead while I filled in the points I'd already listed on the first sheet, hoping that somehow the hours and hours of my life that I'd devoted to looking at pictures of horses, riding and grooming them, watching movies and reading books about them, would be enough to recall another thirty-three little words. I traced my finger over each diagram and filled in the blank lines: number twenty-two — croup; number thirteen — gullet; number forty-five — tendons; then another and another until I had only three blank lines left.

'Number six is *projecting cheek bone*,' said a voice.

Demi stood behind me, watching as I scribbled the answer down.

'And that's the *cleft of frog*,' she said tapping on number fifty-two. 'And the last one's *ergot*.'

I wrote down the last answer and sighed with a mixture of satisfaction and relief. Demi picked up the sheet and took it to her desk. She sat down and took out a red pen and returned a few minutes later with the sheet and a smile. 'All correct.'

'Really?' I was chuffed as a new dam.

'I won't give you those three last answers, but yes, really. That's something of a Linley record. For Year Seven, anyway.'

'Yes!' I cried, punching the air.

Demi frowned. 'Let's not forget where we are, Miss Miller. Fifty correct answers does not mean you're suddenly free of the Linley school code of classroom conduct.'

I giggled. She sounded so formal. Nothing like the way she was out in the arena. I had the feeling she was having some fun at Linley's expense. I had another feeling. That my worksheet had made her a little less mad at me. But only a little.

Demi corrected and returned the rest of the papers, squealing with delight at some, frowning at others and encouraging a few more. I waited for her to present me with some sort of trophy but she had obviously used up her praise quota for the lesson.

'It seems you all know a bit about the outside of a horse,' Demi said to the class. 'But you still have a lot to learn about the inside.'

Demi took a remote control from her desk and pointed it at the classroom ceiling. Instantly the data projector came on and an enormous diagram of a horse's skeleton appeared on the wall. There were words I'd never heard before, like *ulna, humerus* and *mandible,* and other more familiar words, like *pelvis, vertebra* and *cranium.*

'The horse's body is built around its skeleton. Without it the horse would be—'

'Jelly!' a girl named Sandy called out.

Demi smiled. 'True, but in future raise your hand. The horse's skeleton is the framework for his body. Like a house. Anyone ever seen a house being built?'

There were murmurs of 'yes' around the classroom.

'The horse's skeleton works in the same way as the frame of a house. No frame, the roof and walls would collapse. And the interior of the house would be damaged or destroyed.' Demi watched us all carefully, gauging whether or not we understood. 'The skeleton protects the horse's organs. It also helps the horse to move. One of the fascinating things about the equine skeleton is that they actually have two — the axial and the appendicular.'

Sandy raised her hand. 'Axi-what?'

'Axial,' Demi repeated. 'The axial skeleton is the bones of the skull, spine, ribs and sternum. The appendicular skeleton is the bones of the limbs.'

'What are the bones made up of?' I said suddenly. I slapped my hand over my mouth and waved the other hand up in the air.

Demi shot me a look. It was obvious that her joy at my worksheets had worn out. 'Fibrous protein tissue. And minerals like calcium, phosphorus and magnesium. They contain bone marrow, of course.'

India raised her hand daintily. 'What does the bone marrow do?'

'Excellent question, India. And an even more excellent way of asking.' Demi smiled at India, who glowed with delight. 'The bone marrow makes blood cells.'

India raised her hand again and waved it a little. 'How do you know all this, Demi? You're so smart.'

I glared at her over my shoulder, hating her even more than I had that morning, and groaned.

'Got a problem, Ashleigh?' Demi snapped.

I shook my head. 'No.'

'Good. Keep whatever's wrong with you to yourself.'

I stared down at the desk, my face burning with humiliation.

'Now get back to equine physiology,' Demi said, producing another set of handouts from her desk. She thrust the bundle at me. 'Hand these out, please.'

I scraped my chair back and handed a sheet to each girl. India snatched hers with her forefinger and thumb, as though the paper was contaminated, then wiped her hand on her tunic. Her henchgirls cackled.

I sat down at my desk and stared at the paper, reading the passages about ligaments, tendons and muscles over and over again. I learned for the first time that a horse's ligaments take so long to recover from injury because of their poor blood supply. I learned that a horse's tendons act like elastic bands and give them a spring in their step. I learned that a horse's muscles are sensitive and can be very painful when injured due to their good blood supply but heal quickly. I scribbled answers to the questions at the bottom of the sheet in my Horsemanship workbook and concentrated hard on keeping my work neat, my answers correct and my mouth closed.

The bell rang and, as usual, the Linley girls sat still in their seats. Nobody at Linley dared rush out of the classroom door just because the bell had rung.

Demi leaned on her desk and folded her arms. 'For homework, finish the set questions on the worksheet. I want all sheets glued neatly into your books.' I smiled to myself. I'd already done both of those things. I wanted to please Demi. I didn't like her being angry with me.

'And don't forget that your riding lesson starts in an hour so be dressed, tacked up and ready to go in the indoor arena.' Demi gestured towards the door and the class stood up, tucked their chairs under their desks and left the room. She sat back down at her desk and wrote in her big black teaching book.

I was the last to leave, hanging back deliberately to steal a private moment with Demi. I hovered beside her for a minute with so much to say to her that I didn't know where to begin.

'Why are you still here?' Demi said, without looking up.

'I—uh,' I said. 'I—'

'You're in the saddle in fifty-six minutes.' Demi looked up at last. 'So you'd better get a wriggle on.'

I drew in a shaky breath. Didn't she know I still hadn't been given the all clear to ride? Hadn't they told her? I didn't want to bring up the accident so I nodded. 'Okay.'

I sat in the grandstand of the indoor arena watching as the riders warmed up their mounts. There were about eight girls in the group, most of whom I didn't know. Considering Linley was a huge school with over a thousand girls attending from kindy to Year 12, I really didn't stand a haystack in a bushfire's chance of getting to know everyone.

All riders had been graded in first term and classes were now taught in levels. Levels A and B were grouped together for all practical lessons. I was thrilled out of my mind by this as India McCray was the only A level in Year Seven. I'd had to ride a school horse for the gradings and was placed in B level, even though I'd ridden well all last term (apart from nearly killing myself).

India rode her chestnut gelding, Rusty, in a careful, controlled canter around the arena, tightly wrapped in her yellow and green Australian National Youth Equestrian Team jacket. I fantasized for a moment about using it to clean my tack. Or Honey's dock. I couldn't wait until she outgrew it (India and her jacket, not Honey and her dock!). Judging by the rate at which her ego was swelling, it wouldn't take too long. I couldn't believe that she was still at Linley, much less still riding, even more much less riding in A level.

Demi entered the ring leading her tall dun gelding, Cougar, the horse she used for teaching. He was calm and perfect, gazing with gentle dark eyes at the flurry of activity around him.

'Good afternoon, riders!' Demi called. Immediately the level A's and B's sorted themselves into a straight line and settled into the correct seat. I knew what it was like to be out there. I knew what it was like to want to impress Demi more than anything else.

Demi secured Cougar's reins to a loop of twine on the arena fence then approached the line of riders, checking girths, stirrup leathers and throatlashes. She stopped at the end of the line and counted. 'Where's Ashleigh?'

India raised her hand demurely. 'She's not here, Demi.'

Demi grimaced. 'That much is obvious. Does anyone know where she is?'

'I'm here.' I stood up in the grandstand. I wasn't going to hide.

'Where's your horse?' Demi's face was dark. She moved towards me. The line of riders stared.

'In the paddock,' I said.

Demi exhaled sharply. 'May I ask why?'

'I'm not riding today,' I said. My hands started to shake so I shoved one under each arm.

'Out!' Demi cried. She was shrill. It was like she'd been desperate to tell me off, like she finally had an excuse to unleash all the anger I feared she'd been boiling up inside her and now there was no way she could control it. She pointed at the gate of the arena. I could hear murmuring from the riders and felt my face burn. I left the grandstand and stood outside the arena where none of the riders would be able to see or hear.

Demi was right behind me. 'What's going on?' she snapped.

I gulped. 'I can't ride.'

Demi's eyes flashed and she spoke through gritted teeth. 'You know what they say about falling off a horse.'

Something swelled up inside me and before I could stop myself, horrible words were streaming out of my mouth. 'Well, in this case it was your horse and he tried to kill me.'

'Don't even go there, Ashleigh,' Demi spat. 'Thanks to you and your stupidity he could be destroyed.'

I opened my mouth, ready to fight, but Demi beat me to it.

'You had no right to ride my horse. You had no right to use him to sort out your problems. Lightning's in isolation now, in a steel holding yard. I've been waiting for weeks for the School Board to make its decision about whether he's gonna live or die.' Demi's eyes moistened and she took a breath. 'I am so mad with you. I'm just so mad.'

I felt sick instantly. I'd never thought that Lightning could ever be … I shook my head. I didn't want to think about it. 'Why does the School Board have a say?'

'Because the accident happened on school property,' Demi hissed. 'That's why. Because the school has lawyers and powerful parents and insurance premiums and a responsibility to uphold its duty of care. Because the school has a reputation and has to be seen to be doing something.'

'I'm s-sorry,' I said, desperate for it to end. I'd never been spoken to like this before. Not by a teacher, anyway. Demi wasn't exactly what you'd call a regular teacher, but that didn't make it any nicer. All I'd ever wanted was for her to like me and think I was a good rider and to be a part of her world. 'It was India. She made me. She challenged—'

'Oh stop!' Demi said throwing her hands in the air. 'Grow up, Ashleigh. India didn't make you. You made the choice yourself. You could have said no. You could have used your brain. You could have come to me. All this mess would never have happened.'

'But—'

'No!' Demi said. 'I don't wanna hear it. No more excuses. You have got to start accepting responsibility. It's all part of being a horsewoman. And what about your scholarship? Do you really think you can stay at Linley on a riding scholarship and not ride? If you're here to play tennis you play tennis and if you're here to ride you ride. So ride!'

Demi turned her back on me and marched back into the arena. I stood there for a while, stunned, tears running down my face. She hadn't even given me a chance to explain. About India and the doctors and my nightmares. It wasn't fair.

I lay awake in bed again that night, thinking. Thinking about home and how much I was missing it. And thinking about my scholarship. What if they took it away? What then? Would they give it to India, after all? Despite it all, she was a hot rider, the only A level in Year Seven. She'd been at Linley since kindy. I'd have to leave Linley. But how could I face anyone in Shady Creek again?

six

Field of Dreams

'Can you believe what Mrs Freeman said at assembly?' Emily peered over George's withers. She was wearing my black riding helmet — it was a great fit.

I'd agreed to continue giving Em some riding lessons. Just because I wasn't riding in the arena, didn't mean I couldn't teach there!

'I could have done without the whole school lecture about the dangers of riding other people's horses and silly challenges and cyber bullying. I look like a big piece of Swiss cheese under my clothes from all the stares I got. Some of those girls have eyeballs like laser guns.' I pulled upwards on George's girth. I'd shown Emily how to put a saddle blanket on the twenty-five-year-old bay gelding last term. She'd remembered how to place it gently just over his shoulder and slide it down his back in the direction his hair grew. She'd then lowered his saddle onto his saddle blanket and had a go at doing up the girth. 'He's filled his belly with air. In a minute I'll ambush him and take it up another few notches.'

Since Demi's lecture I'd felt better about horses. I'd been to see the school counsellor, Rosie Cooper, and after spending a few hours with her, wished like crazy I'd done it earlier back in Shady Creek. Rosie had put a name to the way I felt — post-traumatic stress disorder. She'd told me that everything that was happening to me was normal after such an accident and that, with the right treatment, I could get it all under control. She taught me some relaxation exercises and talked me through the day of the accident. Reliving it all had been one of the hardest things I'd ever done. I'd cried more than I ever had. I'd had to feel things I'd never wanted to feel again. But at the end of it all, I'd felt better. I'd been back to see Rosie every day since and was finally beginning to feel like the old Ash. Best of all, I hadn't had a nightmare in two whole nights and the tingles had been much better behaved.

'What d'you mean, ambush?'

I giggled. 'I'm not going to jump out from behind him or anything. I'll lead him around for a minute and then do his girth up again. Taking a big breath is a pretty common horsy trick.'

'Why do they do it?'

'How would you like to have a girth around your belly?' I tickled Em's tummy and she laughed aloud.

'I wouldn't really.'

'Well, plenty of horses aren't all that keen on it either.' I rubbed George's mane. He was such a good boy, patient and gentle. The perfect horse for Em to learn on. Strictly speaking she wasn't supposed to be having formal riding lessons until next term, but this wasn't a formal lesson. This was an Ashleigh Miller special. I led George in a circle then tightened his girth three notches! 'Doesn't mean they're being bad. They just wanna be comfortable. Okay, what's next?'

'I give his legs a stretch to make sure there are no folds of skin underneath the girth which could get pinched.' Em said it all quickly, like she wanted to get it out before she forgot.

I watched as Emily lifted each of George's legs just under his knees and stretched them forward gently, then set them down again. 'Brilliant! Now what?'

'Bridle!' Em was my keenest student ever. I'd tried teaching Jenna to ride the summer she'd stayed in Shady Creek. She'd been a good student but wasn't horse mad. Just horse tolerant. Emily Phuong, on the other hand, was certifiably nuts about horses!

'Correct.' I held out George's bridle and Emily took it by the headpiece and examined it for a moment. 'What's up?'

'Exactly,' she said. 'Trying to figure out which end is which.'

I pointed. 'This part you're holding is the headpiece. It goes behind the horse's ears. It splits just below the ears into the cheekpieces and the throatlash.'

'What are the cheekpieces for?'

'They hold the bit in place, see?' I pointed to where the cheekpieces buckled onto two shorter straps which then buckled to the bit. 'The throatlash goes under the horse's throat and does up on the left side. It helps to stop the bridle from coming loose.'

'That can only be a good thing!' Em giggled.

'The browband, see here, it goes across the horse's forehead.' I tapped the browband and smiled to myself, remembering the hundreds of ribbon browbands called Bandies I'd made to raise money for my Horse Cents fund — the cash I earned all by myself to pay for my horses' upkeep.

'Lemme guess — it's for keeping the bridle on as well.' Emily looked triumphant.

'Got it in one, my friend — you're a genius!' I was impressed and nodded approvingly.

'Why, thank you,' Em said, blowing on her fingernails and rubbing them on her jacket.

'Okay, genius, before your head gets too big for my helmet why don't you get that bridle on old Georgie boy.'

'I've only done it once before, you know.' Emily suddenly looked nervous.

I unbuckled George's halter and let it slip down his nose, wrapping the lead rope around his neck in the same move. 'Offer him the bit first. Hold it in your hand then push it against his mouth gently, like you're giving him a slice of carrot.'

Em approached George's nearside and, holding the bridle by the headpiece with her left hand, offered him the bit with her right. He resisted for a moment, then accepted it. 'Yay! I did it.'

'Don't get too excited,' I said. 'You still have to get the headpiece over his ears and buckle up the throatlash.'

Em had George bridled quickly. I clapped my hands in a circle. 'There you go. A round of applause.'

Em held on to George's reins and gave me a look. 'That was probably one of the worst jokes I've ever heard.'

I giggled. 'You still haven't met Pree. I bet you'll change your mind then.'

Em pushed her glasses up on her nose. 'D'you reckon I could meet your friends?'

I gasped and spun in a circle. 'I've had the most incredibly brilliant idea! You can come home with me for exeat! You could meet Becky and Pree, come to Riding Club, I could show you Shady Trails … I just can't believe my own brain sometimes.'

Em's glasses fogged up. That seemed to happen when she got worked up. 'Awesome! A whole blissful, amazing, fantastical weekend without Murky. How can I ever repay you?'

'By mounting George correctly.' I thought for a moment. 'Hey, wouldn't a brotherless weekend be just as fantastical as a Murkless weekend?'

Em shrugged. 'I've told you before. He only grunts and locks himself in his room. I don't notice he's there most of the time.'

'A brother locked in his room,' I said thoughtfully. 'That's what I call a good idea. But knowing Jason I reckon he'd chew through the door eventually. Now, mount!'

Em took a deep breath. 'Okay.'

'Reins over his head. Good. Hold them in your left hand. No, too tight. More loosely. Right.'

'Right hand?' Em said, scrunching up her nose.

'No, left. I meant you did it right,' I said. 'Stand on his left side, facing his tail. Now grab hold of the stirrup with your right hand and turn it outward to face you.'

'Like this?' Em's eyes were wide. The last time I'd given her a lesson I'd done everything for her. This time I was determined that she do it by herself. I knew it was the only way she'd learn.

'Exactly.' I was pleased. Em was a great student. 'Hey, did you know that in some parts of Asia riders use a toe stirrup? It's a loop of rope that's only big enough to hold your big toe. Cool, huh?'

'Is there anything you don't know about horses?'

I laughed. 'Plenty. Okay, put your hand on the far side of the saddle and when you put your foot in the stirrup, I want you to put your weight on it, but be careful — don't dig him in the ribs when you mount. He might think you're asking him to move off.'

'That ever happened to you?' Em bit at her bottom lip.

'For sure!' I laughed again. 'I've wound up hanging upside down from the saddle a few times.'

'Must've taught you to see horses in a whole new way,' Em said, smiling.

'And you thought my joke was bad!' I cried. 'Left foot in the stirrup!'

'Right foot?'

'Under his tummy. You're going to spring off it. One, two …' I watched Em as she bounced on her right foot. 'Three — up! Good! Now swing your right foot over his back — make sure you don't kick him — and lower yourself into the saddle. Yes! You did it.'

I clapped again in the biggest circles I could manage. 'A huge round of applause!'

'No better the second time around, Ash.' Em gave me an even worse look than the last one.

'Comfortable?' I checked George's girth and that Em's stirrups were the right length, then carefully examined her reins. Everything was perfect.

'Very.' Emily had a smile so huge she was lighting up the arena all on her own. 'Now what do I do?'

I had a quick think. 'Last time we went riding we were on a trail. George was happy to follow Honey and Mystery. This time is different. You're going to have to do this on your own.'

Em nodded. 'I'm ready.'

'So we have to make sure you have a good seat. It won't be perfect right away, but try to remember to keep your head up and look between George's ears.' Em listened hard and did her best to follow my instructions. 'Keep your back straight and your shoulders back. Your thighs and knees should be against the saddle — don't grip or squeeze! Good. Balls of your feet in the stirrups, toes pointed forward, heels down — not too far! Good. Em, you look like you were born in the saddle.'

'Next time I talk to Mum I'll ask her. I'm pretty sure she'd remember something like that!' Emily grinned.

'If it was your first time in the saddle I'd lunge you,' I said. 'But you're ready to walk him on your own. You already know how to hold the reins properly.'

Em beamed. 'I was hoping you'd notice. I practise all the time with my Linley hair ribbons.'

'Glad to know they're good for something!' I said, wondering what was wrong with Mrs Phuong's eyesight. Em's short hair wasn't exactly a candidate for ribbons. It was obvious Em had put them to good use. She was holding her hands correctly with her thumbs on top holding the reins and passing them between her thumbs and forefingers as well as her fourth and little fingers.

'I want you to relax and not forget to breathe,' I said.

Em laughed. 'Gimme a break!'

'I'm serious!' I cried. 'Heaps of riders get nervous and don't breathe or they're concentrating so hard they hold their breath. Makes the rider uncomfortable and the horse anxious.'

'So, not only do I have to remember my seat and how to hold my reins, now I have to remember to breathe.' Emily looked cross.

'Breathing is good, Em. Pays to remember to breathe, my friend.' I smiled. 'Squeeze his sides with your lower leg, okay? That's the ask. If he doesn't respond straightaway, apply more pressure. That's the insist.'

George took a step forward.

'You did it!' I was so proud of her. 'Keep the pressure on him with your legs. He'll keep walking until you ask for a transition.'

'A what?' Em stared straight ahead, barely able to control her grin. It looked to me like she was having the time of her life. I felt a tug at my heart. I had never forgotten, could never forget, the first time I'd ridden a horse on my own.

'A transition — the change of pace, you know, from walk to trot and from trot to canter. Don't forget to move your hands with his head and neck and move your bum along with his back. Sort of like you're on a swing.' I watched Em for a moment then realized there was one more thing she needed to know to make a lap of the arena by herself. 'Time to steer. I want you to turn right, so turn your head to the right.'

'Wow upon wow!' Em said. 'It worked.'

'Course it worked.' I followed her around the arena at a safe distance. She was only walking George, but I didn't want to be too close for comfort or too far in case she needed me.

'Done your Latin homework?' Em was so focussed. Except for worrying about Latin homework.

I groaned. 'Maybe if I ignore it it'll go away.'

'That philosophy has let many people down over the course of history, Ash. What do I do if I wanna stop?'

'You apply pressure to his sides and to the reins at the same time.' I watched her carefully. 'Don't yank at his mouth. Gentle pressure is enough.'

'That worked too!' Em said, thrilled with herself as George halted. 'I can help you with your Latin if you like. It's only fair, I mean, you're helping me so much with riding. By the time I have a real lesson I'll be ready for the Olympics!'

I approached George's nearside and took a hold of his bridle. 'Riding — yes. Important — yes. Essential for a girl's survival on the planet — yes. Latin — why? What's Latin got to do with anything?'

'Apart from the Latin word "*equus*", meaning horse, developing into the words "equine" and "equestrian", I guess not a lot.' Em gave me a cheeky smile. 'And then there's that Latin saying that I've heard used so often round these here parts.'

I was instantly curious. 'Which one?'

'*Equus costus muchus!*' Emily laughed aloud.

'Hilarious. You know there's a polocrosse match on this arvo?' I held on to George's reins under his chin. It was time for Em to dismount and for George to have a rub down, a groom and a feed.

Em gave me a look. I was getting a lot of those. 'I go to school here, remember?'

'Remember how to dismount?'

Em beamed. 'Sure do.' Em held onto the pommel and shook her feet out of the stirrups, leaned forward and swung her right leg up and over George's back then dropped to the ground.

'That was awesome, Em!' I said.

Em wrapped her arms around George's neck. 'Horse mad forever?'

I rubbed the sweet gelding's nose. 'Horse mad forever.'

'Ahh, the sweet smell of polocrosse.' I stood between Emily and Ricki in the viewing area of the polocrosse field. It was the first game of the term and the Linley Juniors, my team, were up against pink-shirted Wallaby Hill again. 'So good you could come to see the game, Rick,' I said, straining to see who had taken my place riding Mystery in the team.

'Wouldn't have missed it,' Ricki said, her face bright. She pulled her magic wand from the back pocket of her jeans. 'Gives me a chance to try out my new spell.'

'What're you working on?' Em said, peering over her glasses at Ricki.

Ricki cleared her throat and moved her wand in slow circles. 'Pony tails, saddles and cross-country courses, make India M be allergic to horses!'

Ricki flicked her wand elegantly and the three of us fixed our gazes on India. She was fully decked out in her Linley polocrosse uniform of white joddies, a light blue polo shirt, which had a plastic sleeve sewn onto the back for her number, black boots and a white polocrosse helmet.

Emily looked at her watch. (She was possibly the only Linley girl to wear one. Everyone else used their mobiles to tell the time.) It had been at least thirty seconds since Ricki had cast her spell but India hadn't sneezed even once.

'*Ookakabooka!*' Ricki cried, hacking at the air so hard with her wand in India's direction that it was just a brown blur.

'Maybe it's a time-delay spell,' Em said, pushing her glasses up on her nose.

Ricki's eyes widened and she took a pen and notepad from her jacket pocket. 'Time-delay spell? What a brilliant idea! I'm writing that down in my spell book. Have you ever considered a career in magic?'

'It's on my list,' Em said, smiling. 'So, Ash, you gonna tell us the rules of polocrosse?'

I didn't need much encouragement. I told them about the polocrosse racquet with its long handle and loose net and how it was also called a stick and about the rubber ball and how the sport, one of only three truly Australian sports, was a combination of polo and lacrosse. I told them about the polocrosse field and pointed out the markings, which were similar to a netball court with two goalposts at either end, a semicircle in front of the goalposts and a long line painted right across the field a few metres past the semicircle. They listened, wide-eyed, until an air horn blasted, making them both jump.

'Was that India? Has my spell actually worked?' Ricki kissed her wand.

I laughed. 'That's just the start of the first chukka.'

'Who chucked what?' Em frowned.

'Chukka. A chukka is eight minutes long. It's kind

of like a half in soccer,' I said. 'Except there's between six and eight chukkas per match, not two halves.'

'Why between six and eight?' Ricki said, her eyes fixed on India as she tore across the centre of the polocrosse field. 'Why isn't there a set number?'

'Depends on the age of the players,' I said. 'The younger they are, the less chukkas per game. And you play every other chukka.'

'What do you mean?' Em said, scrunching up her nose.

'There are six players per team,' I said just as Wallaby Hill scored their first goal. 'You get split into two groups. The first group plays a chukka while the second rests, then the second group plays the next chukka and the first group rests.'

'What's it like, Ash? Out there, you know, on the field?' Ricki's eyes were round. She looked amazing with her long curly hair framing her face.

I took a long breath. 'It's hard to explain. It's like you're … you see the ball and you go for it and the horse is underneath you and you score a goal and it's like there's something flowing through your veins. The whole world disappears. You just feel so … it's like, it's like flying.'

'Wow,' said Emily. 'You make me wanna ride even more.'

The chukka was over. Wallaby Hill was ahead one point to nil. India rode past on her way off the field. She pulled Rusty to a halt and looked down at the three of us from his back. Her lips curled into a snarl.

'I warned you not to hang around that loser Ricki, Ashleigh. It rubbed off. Just look at you. You're even more cracked than she is.' India laughed and looked over her shoulder, careful not to be her brat self in front of any teachers or senior girls. 'So pathetic!'

Ricki slapped my arm with her hand. 'I've got it. We saw her in half, just like the greatest magicians do, then reattach the two pieces the wrong way around. You know, stick her head to her bum.'

I burst out laughing. Em collapsed in giggles as well and Ricki was gasping.

'You'd be like … like sticking the two halves of her brain back together!' Emily gulped.

India looked shocked. It was obvious she wasn't used to being served up a humungous taste of her own horrible medicine.

'You guys are so gonna get it,' she spluttered. 'You're all gonna get it.'

'And you are so my hero, Rick,' Em said, taking another gulp of air.

Maryanne James — one of the senior girls and Linley's polocrosse captain, as well as Demi's younger sister and one of my heroes — trotted over on her pure white Camargue gelding, Cavalier (or Cav, for short).

'India, what are you doing?' she said. She looked very cross. 'Second chukka's almost over and you should be with your team discussing strategy and not giggling with the spectators.'

'I—uh …' India stammered.

'Get over to your team,' Maryanne snapped. 'There are a dozen Year Sevens dying for a chance to play for Linley Juniors, you know.'

India's face glowed red. She slipped me one last toxic look and trotted Rusty back to where Year Eight's Cleo Anderson on Dallas and Sarah De Silva on Pixie were waiting. They both looked like a cyclone had blown across their faces.

'How've you been, Ash?' Maryanne said, smiling down at me.

I nodded. 'Good, really good.'

'Back in the saddle soon I hope.' She gave me a wink.

I grinned up at her. 'Hope so!'

'You better be,' Maryanne said. She wheeled Cav around, then looked over her shoulder at me. 'Listen, I heard that Demi lost it with you. You gotta give her time. She's not mean, you know. Just scared.'

I nodded and stared hard at the ground, guilt about what I'd done pressing down on me suddenly. By the time I had the strength to look up again she was gone.

Ricki slipped her arm around my waist. 'Everything'll be all right, Ash.'

Em nodded. 'For sure. We'll figure out a way to save Lightning.'

I gulped and my chest began to hurt. The rotten tingles were back.

The air horn blasted again and the third chukka was on. Linley had a lot of work to do, that was for sure.

My mobile phone beeped. I had a message. I pulled it from my tunic pocket, flipped it open and pressed the button.

'What's it say?' Em asked, craning over my shoulder for a look.

'It's from my mum. She says I'm going to the city for exeat. I have an appointment at the hospital then

I'm staying with Jenna for the weekend.' I texted back 'okay', snapped the phone shut again and jammed it back into my pocket.

'That it?' Ricki asked.

'And I'm her gorgeous worgeous girl. They really need to start hanging around people their own age.'

'Didn't you tell me once that your parents don't believe in baby talk?' Em said, just as Cleo smashed Linley's first goal through the goalposts. 'Whoo-hoo!'

'That wore off once the baby brain set in.'

'You'll find out, won't you?' Ricki squeezed my hand. 'If you can ride again?'

I nodded, the tingles tearing at my heart. 'Yeah. I'll find out.'

'It'll be all right, Ash,' Ricki said. She took her wand out of her pocket again and waved it over my back. '*Oolaalaa falaalaa*, tick tocks of Big Ben, let Ash be okay to go riding again.'

'Thanks, Rick.' I squeezed her hand.

'Horse mad forever?' Em said, pushing her glasses up on her nose.

'Horse mad forever!' we chanted together.

seven

Horse Whispers

'Welcome to the wonderful world of Natural Horsemanship.' Demi James smiled at the Year Seven Horsemanship class.

'Natural Horsemanship?' said Sandy. 'Is there anything unnatural about it? And why is it always "manship"? Why isn't it called "Natural Horse-womanship" or "Horsegirlship"?'

'Natural Horsemanship is another way of saying "horse whispering",' Demi said. She leaned back on her desk, folded her arms and crossed her heels. I was all ears at once. I'd always wanted to learn more about horse whispering. I thought I understood Honey pretty well, but I would have given anything to be the Doctor Dolittle of Linley Heights. 'And it's "Horsemanship" whether you like it or not.'

'This is going to be so much better than Horse Anatomy and Physiology,' India hissed.

'How can you say that?' a cute, dark-eyed girl called Nina hissed back. Nina was sitting next to India. I felt genuinely sorry for her. 'Anything to do with horses is okay by me.'

'Natural Horsemanship isn't a new thing,' Demi said. I leaned forward in my seat, hoping that by edging that little bit closer I would lock every last word she said into my brain. 'It's been around since people first began interacting with horses, thousands of years ago. The term is new, though. It's basically a gentle way of training horses, teaching them without fear or breaking their spirit ... having them grow to trust humans and want to please them, and not simply obey because they're too frightened not to or because they're being dominated.'

Sandy raised her hand. I watched her for a moment. She had bright eyes with long dark lashes and wore her hair in pigtails. I'd had a strict no-pigtail policy since I'd been old enough to figure out that they'd stop me getting a riding helmet on my head. 'I don't get it.'

'Okay.' Demi cleared her throat. 'Are horses predators or prey?'

I shot my hand up, remembering what Joe had said to me when I first started at Linley. 'Prey. Horses are wired to escape from danger and avoid being something's dinner.'

The class roared with laughter, but Demi held her hand up in a 'stop' sign. 'Ashleigh's right. Domesticated or not, horses' instincts haven't changed. They're social herd animals who survive by escaping from danger, not fighting it.'

'Stallions fight,' a girl called Lesley said softly. I'd never heard her speak before.

'That's true,' Demi said. 'They will fight each other and the battles can last for hours, sometimes ending in the death of one of the stallions. This happens when wild stallions are fighting for dominance of a herd of mares.'

Sandy raised her hand again. 'Do horses kill other animals?'

'No,' Demi said. 'Not deliberately anyway. But wild stallions have been known to kill the young foals of the last stallion.'

I was shocked. I'd never thought of horses as killers. 'But why?'

'To remove the last traces of the previous stallion's bloodline and establish their own,' Demi said. 'Horses aren't the only animals to do this.'

'That's disgusting,' I said, feeling sick. 'Totally disgusting.'

'I'm sure you're not the only one of us to feel that way, but it's how nature works.' Demi switched on the electronic whiteboard that also worked as a computer and picked up a black marker pen. She wrote some words on the board: *social, herd, prey*. 'Any other questions before I go on?'

A girl called Georgia raised her hand. I didn't remember seeing her in Horsemanship classes last term and wondered if she was new. 'What do you mean by "social"?'

'For starters, horses like the safety of numbers,' Demi said. She drew an arrow from the word *social* on the board and wrote *safety in numbers* at the end of the arrow. 'Besides that, they enjoy and need the company of other horses and feel lonely and vulnerable on their own, just like humans do. In the wild, even stallions without a herd will band together and live harmoniously. Until a mare turns up, that is.'

'How do horses communicate?' Nina said.

Demi drew another arrow from *social* and scribbled the word *communication* at the end. 'Who can tell me how horses communicate?'

'Neighing!' India said, looking like the pony that got the pellets.

'Vocalization, yes,' Demi said, adding to her notes on the board. 'But compared to other animals who communicate with sound a horse's range vocally is actually quite limited. So what's the main way?'

I was overjoyed (on the inside, of course) to see India deflate a little. I raised my hand.

'Yes, Ashleigh?'

'Body language.' I sat up straight in my seat.

Demi looked pleased. 'Correct.'

The class brainstormed the different ways horses communicate and soon the board was covered with words like *putting ears back*, *showing teeth*, *swishing tails* and *swinging hips*.

'These are all signs that the horse is not happy,' said Demi. 'What about signs that the horse is accepting and relaxed?'

Hands were up and waving frantically.

'Ears forward!'

'Calm eyes!'

'Relaxed nostrils!'

'Soft tail!'

Demi wrote like mad on the board. She smiled at the class. 'By spending time not just riding, but observing your horses, you'll understand much more about the way they communicate and what they're trying to say. Each horse will have his or her own way of responding in a particular situation. Some will be more anxious than others, some more curious, some more playful. Horses are as individual as we are. It's important to learn to read their behaviour. It's the only way, really, to begin to understand how they feel and what they think.'

'What's all this got to do with Natural Horsemanship?' India said.

Leave it to India.

'Everything. Natural Horsemanship is communicating with horses their way. A practitioner would hope to have a similar relationship with her horse that her horse may have with another horse in the wild.'

'That's impossible!' India snorted derisively. I waited for Demi to explode but she merely shook her head.

'It's not. Horses use all those behaviours we talked about to communicate and increase those behaviours if they need to get a message across. By using similar body language, a trainer can get a horse to respond to and respect them.'

There were murmurs of 'ohhh' around the room.

'Year Seven, pick up your books and a pen. We're going for a walk,' Demi said.

We all looked around the room at each other then slowly scraped back our chairs.

'We've talked about the ways that horses communicate and the body language they use. Now we're going to see it for ourselves.'

I so loved Horsemanship. Instead of being at our desks, taking notes and doing worksheets, here we were at the riding centre, leaning on the post-and-rail fences with our elbows, gazing out at the mares' paddock. Honey was grazing at the bottom of the paddock, Rose by her side. I could see, even from the fence, that her rug was secure and I was relieved.

'Mares are interesting to watch in a herd. Does anyone know who the leader of a herd is?' Demi watched the class, who murmured together.

'Um,' said Sandy. 'The stallion?'

'That's usually what people think,' Demi began. 'But you may be surprised to learn that it's often an older mare. A lead mare keeps the herd under control, chooses the best spots for grazing and drives away troublesome horses. She's smart and respected by the herd and is responsible for them when the stallion is away.'

I was surprised. So Fly Eyes was the leader of this herd. I'd have thought that a stallion would have sorted her out in a hoofbeat. But obviously she'd been the one doing the sorting. Maybe she wasn't as mean as I'd thought. Maybe she had her herd's best interests at heart and was only ever trying to protect them from predators like me!

I thought about Lightning. What had it been like for him to be ridden by a stranger while dozens of girls watched and screamed? Had I even once stopped to think about the day of the accident from his point of view? Goose bumps broke out all over my arms as it hit me like a barrel of molasses. I'd been a bad horsewoman that day. Lightning had been acting on pure instinct and I'd used none.

'A horse wants to be accepted by the herd and each horse has a place in the herd. When a new mare joins a herd she has to find her place and a friend.' Demi gestured to the paddock. 'When you look out there, what do you see?'

'Der,' India muttered. 'Horses.'

'Correct, India,' Demi said. 'And ten points from your house for your "der".'

India's face went purple but she squeezed her lips shut tight. I grinned, inside again.

'What do you notice about the horses?' Demi said. 'Look hard.'

The class was silent. Finally Lesley raised her hand. 'They're in pairs.'

Demi beamed. 'Correct! Mares will usually pair off with other mares and form deep friendships. They'll even groom each other.'

'Wow,' I said. I was loving every minute of this lesson. I so wanted to understand Honey. There was so much I didn't know about her. Who had been her dam? Where had she been born and on which exact date? Who had cared for her and broken her in and trained her? How had she wound up on a run-down, dusty farm? Had someone loved her before the cruel people I'd rescued her from?

'Year Seven — observe and take notes!'

I flipped open the exercise book I was carrying and took a pen from my tunic pocket, then sat on the grass just outside the fence. I watched the herd and scribbled notes, while Demi patrolled the class. I was soon lost in the world of horses, the only world I wanted to be in, that I'd ever wanted to be in. I watched as Honey grazed alongside Rose and saw Rose rub at her neck. Fly Eyes grazed with two other mares and looked up every now and then and surveyed her herd. When she moved, the other mares followed. Some of the mares were lying down, while others stood with their heads low, sleep-like. Two mares cantered playfully across the paddock together. It seemed a safe, structured community.

'The key to having a good relationship with your horse and kick-starting your dazzling careers as horse whisperers is trust. Horses don't like to be separated from their herd, so they need to know that when they are with you they'll be safe. And what do you think is the best way to gain your horse's trust, Year Seven?' Demi scanned the faces of her class.

I raised my hand. 'Spending time with her?'

Demi nodded. 'Anything else?'

'Patience,' Lesley said in a voice so low she was almost whispering.

'Yes, and?'

Georgia raised her hand. 'Being calm?'

Demi nodded again. 'And?'

'Understanding the way a horse thinks.' India looked thoughtful. Maybe she'd learned as much as I had today.

'Brilliant!' Demi said. 'You're all brilliant.'

In order to avoid seventeen serious cases of head inflation from being told how brilliant we were, the class was set two chapters on horse communication and body language to read and summarize. There was only one thing that was going to keep me going in the face of two whole chapters, plus four pages of Maths, a rough draft of an original narrative and the beginnings of a History research assignment on Ancient Egypt — a taste of Honey!

'You're my good girl,' I said, running my hands over my horse's face. We were together, alone in her stall. I wanted everything that Demi had said. I wanted her to trust me, to love me. I wanted to be as important to her as she was to me.

It had been weeks since I'd sat on her back. Nearly eight weeks in fact. I'd been doing all the exercises that my physiotherapist had told me to do. I'd avoided all back-damaging activities like contortionism, kick-boxing and flying trapeze work just like a horse avoids a patch of grass he's pooed on. I'd sorted the tingles out and they seemed to have finally left me alone. I'd done everything right. Now all I had to do was get the all clear from the doctors at the Children's Hospital in the city and I'd be a rider again.

I ran my hands down her neck and over her withers then rested them on her smooth back at the place I used to sit, the place that connected me to her, and felt the warmth of her body flow into mine. It was like electricity. I shivered. She turned her head and nudged my bottom, like she was telling me it was okay to ride her. I knew she must have been confused and maybe even wondering what she'd done wrong. I'd been with her every day for a year and a half, and then suddenly I was gone and a stranger was feeding and grooming her. Then I'd come back out of the blue, all scared and jittery, and didn't ride her.

'I'm so sorry,' I whispered. It wasn't hard now to think from her perspective. I realized then just exactly how much I'd missed out on and how much I'd missed her. I wondered if she'd missed me too. She would've missed the treats and extra long grooms and the cuddles, I was pretty sure of that. I realized something else. Honey had never let me down, not on purpose, anyway.

'It won't be much longer, Honey,' I said, burying my face in her perfect copper-coloured coat. It was thicker now, growing in for winter despite the rug. I'd given her a good groom and was thankful to the horse gods that I'd spent part of my Horse Cents money on a light bib for her to wear underneath her rug so that the buckles didn't rub her coat away at her shoulders. She looked beautiful.

'Everything's going to be okay,' I murmured, breathing in her scent. 'They'll let me ride again. And when they do, you just wait and see. We'll show them all.'

eight

Wedding Belles

'So what'd they say?' Jenna said as I slid into the back seat of her mum's car. Mrs Dawson was chatting with my parents in the hospital car park. She hugged my mum, kissed Jason's chubby hand and threw my overnight bag in the boot. They were spending the night at Grandma's and I was on loan to the Dawsons.

Jenna's blue eyes were wide. They looked even bigger now that her hair was cropped so short. It suited her, though.

I beamed. 'They gave me the all clear. I can ride again.'

Jenna offered me her palm for a high-five. 'Yes!'

I slapped her hand with mine, just as her mum started up the car. 'I really wanna ride again, Jen.'

As we drove away, I waved to my family through the rear windscreen.

'That's such great news. It'll be nice to have the old Ash back. You're just not you without horses,' Jenna said, grinning.

'But you always hated horses,' I said, turning to look out the window for a while. Everything seemed so big and busy and crowded. I was born and grew up right here in this city. But it all seemed so long ago and so far away.

'I never hated horses!' Jenna protested. She grabbed my arm and I turned back to her. 'Okay, I might have said that once or twice, but I never really meant it. They stink a bit, though.'

'So does perfume!' I said, laughing. 'Anyway, the smell's one of the best parts.'

'Smell or no smell, I still want you riding again. You need to be you, Ash.' Jenna flashed her braces at me. 'I'd rather you were happy and smelly than miserable and as boring as you've been.'

'Thanks a lot!' I cried, play-whacking her.

'You two knock it off,' Mrs Dawson said. I'd forgotten she was driving the car. 'Any more trouble and I'll be pulling this car over and it will be *uno schiaffo grande per voi due!*'

'Yeah right, Mum. You won't give us a big smack.' Jenna leaned over the seat and planted a kiss on her mum's cheek. Mrs D had changed so much since the last time I'd seen her. Her hair was long and blonde, she was wearing make-up and she seemed so smiley. I hadn't remembered her like that at all. Jenna hadn't been the only one to change during those six months in Italy. I smiled to myself remembering the new and not at all improved Jenna when she'd come to stay in Shady Creek after her holiday in Italy. She'd acted like an alien from planet Brat and it had taken some serious horse therapy to sort her out.

'How far to your house?' I asked.

'Another five minutes,' Mrs D said. 'We're really close to the hospital. It'd be two minutes without all this rotten traffic. Hey — *stupido! Dove hai imparato a guidare?*'

'*Where'd you learn how to drive?*' Jenna nudged me and stifled a giggle. 'She learned how to road rage in Italian while we were in Rome.'

'How's *your* Italian going?' I asked her, my eyebrows arched.

Jenna rolled her eyes. 'Don't remind me what a creep I was! But I learn it at school and I get to practise at home.'

I'd never been to Jenna's new place before. Just after we'd moved to Shady Creek, Jenna's parents had split up. They'd sold their house and both bought new units close to the city centre. I thought about all the times Jenna and I had hung around in her room and how we'd built barricades against her door to keep her horrible twin brothers out and how we'd only be coaxed out by the smell of the cookies that Jenna's dad loved to bake. I knew I'd never go to her place and see her mum and dad together again and I felt a little sad for Jenna. But then I watched her chatting with her mum about clothes and shopping, and she didn't look sad. She looked fine, the same as she'd looked before except for the haircut, make-up and braces.

'Here we are, Ash,' Jenna said. I craned for a look at her building.

Mrs D turned the car into a driveway underneath a tall block of new units. She pulled a remote control from her handbag and pushed a button.

A garage door opened and we drove inside, under the building. Jenna's mum pulled into a parking spot that said '20'. There was another parking spot for '20' right beside it.

'We're home!' Jenna said. 'I can't believe you're here!'

We tumbled out of the car and I grabbed my bag from the boot. Jenna pulled me towards a door by my hand. She heaved against the door and dragged me up two flights of stairs, then pulled a key from a chain around her neck and opened the door of Unit 20. 'Home, sweet home!'

'You got the door, Jen?' Mrs D called from downstairs.

'Yeah!' Jenna hollered.

I followed her inside, straight into a tiled hallway. The unit was cool and dark inside. Jenna flicked a switch and the hallway was flooded with light. 'I'll give you the big tour.'

Jenna knocked on a closed door. 'That's Mum and Ant's room.'

'Your mum has ants in her room?' I gaped at my best friend.

Jenna threw back her head and laughed. 'No, silly. Ant is Antonio. You remember? Mum's boyfriend.'

'Oh.' I had remembered. Of course I'd remembered. But I hadn't expected that he lived with them here too.

'Straight down there, see, that's the kitchen,' Jenna said, passing a doorway. She turned left and I followed her down another long hallway. 'And that's the bathroom, and the office.'

We stopped outside another closed door. Jenna gave me a look. 'This is the brats' room. I wanted them up front where Mum and Ant are. But no, she had to put them here, right next to me. I can't get any peace, I swear it. And the pong comes into my room.' Jenna opened the door to reveal the messiest bedroom I'd ever seen. Toys and clothes and DVD cases were strewn across the floor and the bunk beds were unmade. There was a TV, which had been left on, a game station on the floor and model planes and spaceships hanging from the ceiling. The smell was interesting to say the least. Old yucky socks and stale milk.

'Pee-yew!' I said.

'Pee-yew is right,' Jenna closed the door and took a deep breath. 'Fresh air — thank goodness!'

The last door was straight ahead. Jenna gestured towards it proudly. 'My room. Go on, open the door.'

I twisted the doorknob and pushed the door open. 'Wow.'

The room was gorgeous.

One whole wall was a glass double door which opened onto a huge balcony. The blinds were open and I could see plants and a barbecue and an outdoor setting and bikes. There was a small table in the corner and I could see by the paintings hanging up on a fold-away clothes hoist that the boys used it for art and craft. There was even a little sandpit, a lounge and two hammocks. It was like an oasis.

Jenna had a brand-new double bed with a shimmering, satin doona cover that looked like it had come from India. She had a pink desk and chair, a computer and a built-in wardrobe with double mirror sliding doors. There was a bookshelf, with all her books arranged neatly according to colour and size, and framed photos mounted on the walls. I noticed one of her and me when we were still at school together. Our arms were around each other and we were grinning at the camera. There was a huge photo of Jenna with her dad as well. I gasped when I noticed a mirror ball hanging from the ceiling and realized that someone, probably her mum, had lovingly painted clouds and rainbows on the powder blue walls. It was the most beautiful bedroom I'd ever seen.

'So, whaddya think?' Jenna collapsed on her bed and sprawled out on her stomach.

I threw myself down next to her. 'It's awesome. Just totally amazingly awesome! Bit different, though.'

Jenna wrinkled her nose. 'How do you mean?'

'Your old room was nothing like this.' I scratched at my knee. 'Do you miss it? Your old place?'

Jenna rolled onto her back and stared at the ceiling. 'I did heaps at first, you know? I didn't want anything to change. I know this girl at school whose parents are divorced as well but her dad gave her mum the house. She never had to move.'

'Does she see her dad?' I summoned up my incredible telepathic abilities and used them to order the lump that was starting to rise in my throat to go back where it came from.

'Every second weekend,' Jenna said simply. 'She stays at his place with her sister.'

I swallowed. 'What about your dad? Do you see him?' I tried to tread carefully, knowing not to push Jenna too hard. She'd never really liked to talk about the divorce. When her parents had first split up she'd begged me not to tell anybody.

Jenna rolled back onto her tummy and picked at her doona cover. She swung her feet in the air. 'All the time. I sleep over every second weekend. Mum and Dad get along now that everything's all over. He picks us up from school and brings us back here when Mum's at work and babysits if she needs him to.'

'Every what's all over?'

Jenna gave me an incredulous look. I felt small and babyish. 'The divorce! The settlement, all that stuff. It's all I heard about for ages but now they both have what they want they don't argue anymore. Not in front of me, anyway.'

I prayed to the horse gods that I was about to say the right thing. 'Does your dad have a girlfriend?'

Jenna nodded. 'Yep. Michelle.'

'What's she like?' I asked. I bit at my bottom lip.

'Nice,' Jenna said casually. 'She takes me shopping sometimes and leaves the brats with Dad for man-to-man time. She promised me she'll teach me how to knit as well. I wanna make a scarf for school with all different colours in it.'

'You're allowed to wear a scarf like that to school?' I said, thinking about the uniform demerits at Linley Heights School.

Jenna laughed. 'No! But I want one anyway.'

There was a loud noise at the front door. I could hear Mrs D and a man speaking Italian and high-pitched little-boy voices.

'Come and meet Ant!' Jenna jumped up from the bed, grabbed my hand and tugged. I remembered when she'd first told me about him, she'd rolled her eyes and chewed her gum. But now she seemed excited he was home.

My tummy flip-flopped. What was he like? I couldn't imagine anyone but Mr D being the man in Jenna's house. I remembered him in the kitchen wearing his Kiss the Cook apron and wondered if I'd ever see him again. But I let her drag me from the bed and down the hallway to the kitchen.

The kitchen was one of those white sparkling clean ones with silver appliances that I'd only ever seen on TV. There was a tall man with dark curly hair twirling Jenna's mum around the floor in his arms. He had a long-stemmed red rose in his hand and was singing at the top of his lungs, something about 'amore'. Mrs D was giggling, her face flushed with delight. Toby and Max, Jenna's total pain seven-year-old twin brothers, shrieked with glee and clapped their hands. They looked nothing like each other except for their bright green eyes, but they were completely identically annoying.

'Ash-a-lee,' Max burped as soon as he saw me.

Toby roared with laughter then shoved his hand under his armpit and flapped his arm like a chicken. 'Check this out!'

'Armpit fart!' Max jumped up and down. Mrs D and Antonio stopped dead. Antonio grabbed Toby from behind and tipped him upside down, then right-side up again. Toby giggled and Max cheered.

'No more of the silly businesses in front of your sister's friend!' Antonio said, his handsome face breaking into a huge grin. He spoke English with an accent. 'Giovanna! Is this the famous Ash-a-leigh?'

'*Si*,' Jenna said. 'Ash, this is Antonio.'

Antonio offered me his hand. I took it and he shook mine warmly.

Mrs D ran her fingers through his hair tenderly and I noticed something for the first time. She was wearing a huge sparkling ring on her wedding finger.

'Double wow,' I said. 'That's the biggest rock I ever saw.'

'Didn't you tell Ash yet, Jen?' Mrs D said, incredulous. 'I thought you two would be looking at bridesmaids' dresses by now. What'd you do with all those magazines I gave you?'

'You're getting married?' I asked.

Mrs D nodded, glowing, and snuggled into Antonio's arms.

'Giuseppina is the love of my life,' Antonio said, kissing the top of Mrs D's head. 'The most beautiful woman I have ever known.'

'Love words!' Jenna said, rolling her eyes. 'Honestly, if you're gonna do that can't you at least do it in Italian so we don't have to suffer?'

Antonio and Mrs D laughed, then kissed on the lips. Jenna tugged on my arm and dragged me back to her room, closing the door behind us.

'I need you to be there, Ash. Please, for me? Everyone'll be looking at me. I can't do this without you.' Jenna's eyes were wide and urgent.

'When's the wedding?' My head was spinning.

'Next holidays.' She lay on her bed again and rubbed at her eyes. 'I can't believe I'm gonna be my mum's bridesmaid!'

I sat beside her. 'What about the boys?'

'They can't be bridesmaids. They're boys. They'd have to be bridesboys. They'd look pretty stupid in a dress.'

'No, what are they gonna be?'

Jenna sat up, blinking. 'They're giving her away. Cute, huh?'

I nodded, unable to imagine anything less cute than Max burping 'I do' and Toby armpit-farting the wedding march. 'Why doesn't your nonno give her away?'

'Mum said he's had his turn already and how many kids get to give their mums away at weddings? Besides, you know Nonno lives in Italy.'

'Oh yeah,' I said, feigning dumbness. I grinned. 'This is so cool. I mean, how many kids get to be their mum's bridesmaid?'

Jenna covered her face with her hands. 'So far, I think I could be the only one.'

'I'm sure you're not.' I sat beside her and smoothed down the doona cover. 'Hey, what's Ant's last name?'

'Ciciarri.'

'Josephine Ciciarri. Sounds nice, Jen.'

'Thanks!' Jenna sighed and lay back again.

'Hey, Jen?' I said softly. I had to talk to her about this whole horse thing. At that moment she was the only one whose opinion really mattered to me.

'Yeah?' Jenna turned onto her side and watched me earnestly with her blue eyes.

'You know me and riding?'

Jenna rolled her eyes. 'Are you kidding? Exactly how long have we been friends now?'

I thought for a moment. 'Well, you know how they gave me the green light to ride again?'

Jenna's face was suddenly serious. 'Yeah. And you said you really wanted to ride.'

'I do,' I began. 'But what if I can't do it anymore? What if I've forgotten how? What if Honey rejects me? What if I've changed?'

Jenna sat up, facing me. She grabbed my hand and squeezed it. 'Changes happen, Ash. Things'll change and be different all the time, but that doesn't mean they can't be good.'

'But what if I suck at riding now?'

'Then you'll train hard. You'll try your best to do better and better until you don't suck.' Jenna smiled. She made it sound so simple.

'But what if I train hard and I still suck. What if no matter what I do I'm never the rider I used to be?' I could feel the tears coming. I was so afraid. Not of horses, not anymore. But of not being able to do the thing I'd been born to do. Of not being the person I wanted to be.

'Then you ride anyway, because it's what you

love,' Jenna said. She was still holding my hand. I felt blessed by the horse gods to have a friend like her.

'But what if I ride differently?'

Jenna gestured around the room with her free hand. 'I live differently now. But I'm still me. Things changed in my life, but the changes didn't change me. You're still the same person, Ash. No accident can ever change you. You might feel different and for a while there you looked different!'

I play-whacked her, thinking of how I must have looked in the hospital bed with all those tubes and mess of unbrushed hair. 'Don't remind me!'

'But on the inside you're still you. And on the inside you're totally horse mad. Right?'

I squeezed her hand and smiled. 'Right.'

I realized then that Jenna was the most amazing person, the bravest person ever. She'd survived the changes and was taking everything that life threw at her in her stride, the way I had always wanted to. If she could do it, I could. I knew then it was time. It was time to ride again. It was time to be the person I was meant to be. I thought about Honey and school and polocrosse and Demi and I couldn't wait for it all to begin.

nine

Back Where I Belong

It was early morning. Mist hung over the paddocks, the grass was crisp and wet and the horses blew smoky breath as they grazed.

It was time.

My lead rope was coiled like a snake and was slung over my shoulder. My riding boots felt stiff and strange on my feet as I walked towards the paddock. I had on a new pair of navy-blue joddies, which felt tight around my knees. I rubbed my cold hands over them, feeling the ridges under my fingers, and thought about how comfy my old pair had been before they'd been cut from my body with a pair of sterilized silver scissors. I had a moment of panic, wishing I'd asked someone to keep them for me. But the blood …

Honey was waiting alone by the paddock gate. It was like she knew. I clipped the lead rope under her chin and unhooked the gate.

'Morning, beautiful girl,' I said, rubbing her forelock. She nuzzled my hand for a treat. I didn't let her down. There was a slice of carrot waiting in my palm. She crunched gratefully and followed me from the paddock.

Linley was still. I felt like I was the only person on Earth. I led Honey to the stables. For the first time in months, my saddle, bridle and saddle blanket were hanging over the rails of Honey's stall. I'd never felt so full of purpose. I'd ridden at State level, competed at Waratah Grove Riding Academy and won a scholarship to Linley Heights School, but I'd never felt like I did at that moment. I was going to ride my horse. I was going to be one with her again. I was going to get my life back. This wasn't about a ribbon or a trophy or beating anyone. It wasn't about times or knocking down rails or perfect grooming. It wasn't about anything but being me, being the person I was born to be. It was about being a rider.

I unrugged and groomed Honey. She hadn't had her breakfast, but I knew it was best to feed her after our ride. I settled her saddle blanket on her back. It brought back so many memories. I'd used that saddle blanket at Shady Creek Riding Club, at Shady Trails, at Waratah Grove, at gymkhanas and shows. I wasn't the same girl I'd been before the accident. But I was using the same gear. These things, all these things, were like something from a time capsule — familiar in one way but at the same time they seemed to be from another life. I saddled Honey, bridled her and led her from her stall. No riding was allowed in the stables (or any stables for that matter), so I had to wait just a few moments longer.

I steadied Honey just outside the stables and pulled her reins over her head. My pulse throbbed, like life was pumping back into my body. The world was silent, like it was holding its breath. I held her near stirrup and pushed my left foot into it. I hadn't done this in so long. It had been as natural to me as walking, but I hadn't made my body stretch like this for too long. The physiotherapy had been one thing, but having to shove my foot into a stirrup that hung at chest height was a whole different mounted game.

I held on tight to Honey's reins, careful though not to yank, and twisted a handful of her mane into my fingers. I was conscious not to pull myself up by her pommel, but rather to spring from my right foot. I took a deep, slow breath. This was it. I had a hold of my horse's reins and one foot in the stirrup. I either mounted and took a firm hold of who I used to be, or walked away and left everything I had ever known behind.

Honey stood patient and calm as she had ever been. She knew I needed time, I needed to do this when I was ready. I trusted her and I knew she trusted me. There was no fear and there were definitely no tingles. I bounced on my right foot and sprang into the saddle, settling down gently on Honey's back. It was only then that I took another breath, a smile spreading over my face. Honey turned her head to gaze up at me. She seemed content that I was right where I should be.

'We did it,' I said softly, rubbing at her mane. 'Thank you. Thank you, Honey.'

I sat for a while, settling into my saddle and watching as Linley came slowly to life. Joe started up his tractor and headed off to do the morning feed. Horses trotted beside him along the fence, whinnying in greeting (and joy that it was breakfast time!). I laughed aloud with the sheer delight of it and gathered my reins. It was time to ride, time to be a rider. It was time to be me.

I sat outside the counsellor's office alone, wriggling in my chair and fidgeting with a horsy magazine. Her door was closed and the green ribbon was tied on the door handle, letting me know that someone was with her and I would have to be patient. I had to talk to her. Rosie had helped me so much, I had to tell her about my ride. I had to tell her everything I'd done and seen and what it had been like to feel like myself again. I had to tell her that I was going to be okay.

The door opened suddenly and I jumped to my feet. Rosie was in the doorway, murmuring to a girl whose eyes were red. The girl sniffed and rubbed at her blotchy face with a crumpled pink hanky.

'Claire!' I gaped at her, shocked. 'What are you doing here?'

Claire Carlson cleared her throat and smoothed her bushy brown hair. Her nose was running. I had never seen her looking so unhygienic. 'None of your beeswax.'

I shrugged, any hope I'd had of getting any closer

to figuring her out thrown in the bin like a soggy tissue. 'Fine.'

Claire looked me up and down, disgust spreading across her face. 'You've been riding, haven't you? What is it with you and *horses*?' I was stung by the way she'd said my favourite word, like it was something dirty, shameful and rude. She turned to Rosie, who was watching us intently. I could almost see the germ of a doctoral thesis morphing inside her head. 'Rosie, tell her to have a shower before she comes into our room. I can't stand the smell, I just can't stand it!'

'I'm not the one who has problems with horses, Claire,' I spat. 'It's you. Why can't you be normal?'

Claire's dark eyes widened and filled with tears. 'Horses ruined my life. Oh, no!' She suddenly looked scared, like she'd said the wrong thing. Like she'd peeled back the bandage on her heart just enough so that I might get a glimpse inside and begin to know her. I'd lived with Claire long enough to understand that the last thing she wanted was for anybody to be close to her.

'Ashleigh!' Rosie said. I'd almost forgotten she was there. 'That was unkind. Apologize to Claire.'

I knew I'd crossed the line, but I didn't want to

admit it. I thought for a second, about myself. I knew I was an okay person, but there were things about me that needed to change. The horsemadness could stay. My allergy to the word 'sorry' needed treatment. Later. 'Why doesn't she apologize to me? She said I stink!'

Rosie gestured towards the door of her office. 'Maybe you should both come inside.'

I shook my head. I wasn't going to let Claire see inside me. She might be a bandage ripper, but I wasn't going to be. 'No way. Not with her.'

'Claire?'

Claire shook her head, her lips squeezed tight. She folded her arms across her chest and stared at the floor. She sighed and stared up at the ceiling. 'I—'

'Yes,' Rosie urged. 'What do you want to say?'

I watched Claire watching the ceiling. What had she said earlier? What had she said about horses? They'd ruined her life? But how? She'd made no secret of the fact that she hated horses from the very first day I'd been at Linley. But it was the germs she hated, the smell, the poo. Sure, they took some getting used to but they were hardly what anyone would classify as life-ruiners. Standing there like that, all her pain there for anyone to see, she looked so sad and scared that it was impossible for me to be mad with her. All of a sudden I wanted her to stay and talk. It was time to call a truce, to agree to disagree on horses and disinfectant. We were roommates after all.

'I … I'm going now,' Claire said softly. She turned and was gone before either Rosie or I could try to change her mind.

I looked at Rosie and braced myself, expecting her to be furious. Instead she smiled and gestured again towards the door.

I settled myself into one of her comfy armchairs while she made a call to the dorm to make sure that Claire had made it back okay.

'What's wrong with Claire?' I said once Rosie was finished with her call.

'I can't discuss that with you, Ash,' Rosie said simply. 'If you two had come inside together … well, who knows?'

'But she's so hard to live with,' I groaned.

Rosie shrugged. 'Try every now and then to imagine how hard it can be for her to live with you.'

My mouth dropped open. 'I'm not that bad!'

Rosie shook her head. 'That's not what I meant. Of course you're not bad. But neither is Claire. Not everyone thinks the way you do, Ash. Your way of thinking isn't necessarily the right way. Neither is mine nor Claire's. It's okay to think differently, to be different, to like different things. It's okay for you and it's okay for her. You don't have to be the same as other people and it's possible to be friends with people who aren't necessarily like you.'

I let her words soak in for a moment. 'All my friends love horses. All of them.'

Rosie smiled. 'All of them?'

I thought about Jenna. 'Okay, one of them doesn't.'

'But you still became friends?'

I nodded. 'Best friends.'

'Everyone has a story, Ash. Their story, their experiences, shape who they are. Before you rush to judge people, take some time to learn their stories. You might just find yourself making some new friends.'

It was like a tack room light had been switched on inside my head. 'Why don't they teach us stuff like this in school?'

Rosie smiled. 'Life can't be taught. It can only be lived and learned. Now, how was your first ride?'

ten

The Good, the Bad
and the Footy

'I can't believe this is it.' I looked around me at the members of Shady Creek Riding Club. 'What happened?'

It was lunchtime and we were sitting on our logs and upturned milk crates under the triangle of trees that was our 'outdoor clubhouse' but which was now serving as our boardroom. Our horses were untacked and corralled or grazing nearby. I actually had a horse: Cassata, the gorgeous Appaloosa mare, was on loan to me from Rachael Cho (pain big sister extraordinaire) and Becky and I were going to return her unharmed on pain of death.

We'd spent the morning doing warm-up exercises followed by some polework on the ground and graduated to some cavaletti — jumps made from two 'X' shapes with a red-and-white pole between them. The cool thing about cavaletti is that by flipping them over you can lower or raise their height, and you can stack them to make the jumps heaps bigger. They were cheap, too. Gary had made all our cavaletti from old timber. I loved jumping and had competed in cross-country championships. But that was on Honey. On Cassata, having only just been back in the saddle for a couple of weeks, cavaletti were just fine.

'Footy season.' Becky snorted, a disgusted look on her face. She handed out clear plastic bags of prawn chips. 'Most of the boys've nicked off.'

'Soccer? Rugby?' I licked my lips and took a handful of chips then stuffed them into my mouth. Yum.

Becky shook her head. 'Aussie rules. Seriously, who'd choose a fat lump of leather over a horse?'

'Nommee!' Not only did I have a mouthful of half-eaten prawn chips, I was in shock. Shady Creek Riding Club numbers had dropped off by at least a third. Not only had the new boy disappeared, succumbing to the lure of the goalposts, but even

Ryan Thomas, El Creepo Number Three, had traded his riding boots for footy boots. What had happened to gentle-hearted Arnie, Ryan's huge grey gelding? I swallowed and shuddered. 'I meant "not me". It's weird, just weird.'

'Tell me something I don't know. But seriously, why didn't *he* leave?' Becky pointed straight at Flea, not caring for even a nanosecond about how rude finger number two could be when aimed directly at another human being.

Flea was sprawled on a log, Carly by his side as usual. He looked a little less terrifying to me now that his second mate had abandoned ship, and especially now that I'd seen the blue of his eyes. His first mate was still on duty though, and he laughed aloud. 'Couldn't think of a better way to meet girls!'

Becky and I pretend-vomited into our riding gloves and the younger riders giggled. Flea and girls … yuck!

'And yuz better watch whatcha say about footy,' Flea barked. 'Go Wombats!'

I raised my eyebrows, totally unimpressed. 'Go who?'

'Wombats. The Shady Creek Footy Club.' Becky patted my back. 'So young and so much to learn.'

I giggled. 'Wouldn't Dingbats have been a better name?'

Flea's face went purple. 'We smashed Pinebark Ridge Pythons last weekend 12.6 (78) to 2.3 (15), so close your trap, Spiller, or I'll—'

'You'll what?' I sneered. 'Sick a wombat onto me? Oooh, I'm so scared.'

Carly rolled her eyes and smoothed down her Shady Creek Riding Club jumper. It was the first time I'd seen her since she'd tried to run me down with Destiny. I didn't think I'd ever like her. She was neat and shiny and cold as a bandicoot's bum on an August morning in Melbourne. 'So puerile.'

'Can we get onto business?' Becky said. This was serious. It was about saving the club and we all knew it. 'I called this meeting because we're facing a crisis.'

Carly sucked in her cheeks and clapped her hands. 'Great speech!'

'Do you wanna club or not?' Becky snapped.

Carly snapped as well — snapped her mouth right shut.

'We need to get our members back or get new ones,' Becky continued. 'It's not just a matter of money, although club dues really help. It's competing as well. Most age groups won't be able to raise a single team if this keeps up. We won't qualify for any teams events at this rate.'

'Whoa,' I said, doing a quick head count. Twenty-seven. They were mostly Under 10s and Under 12s. Under 14s and up were seriously low on numbers and, apart from Flea, were all girls. 'Is this everyone?'

'Julie and Jodie are in town, doing a shoot.' Becky squeezed her eyes shut and shook her hands. She was flustered and I couldn't blame her. Riding Club was her life. Her dad was the coach and though he was always busy cooking at the restaurant, he loved horses and Riding Club and would do anything for any of the Shady Creek riders at the drop of a riding hat. If the club went under once and for all it would break his heart, and as for Becky … I couldn't bear to think about it.

'Shoot?' I was confused. Things changed so much while I was away I needed a month-long exeat to catch up on all the gossip. Two nights just wasn't enough.

'Modelling,' Becky said. 'Twins. Long story. Tell you later.'

'So, whadda we gonna do, girls?' Flea lounged on his log like a lordly Lipizzaner. He surveyed the group, pointed to the sky and belched. I couldn't imagine what had come over him the last time I was at Riding Club. Maybe he'd had a knock on the head that morning that had temporarily reversed the one he'd had as a baby.

'Firstly we're gonna try to teach you some table manners—' Becky began.

'What're you going on about?' Flea mock-cried. 'This is a log. I don't need manners.'

'Then we're gonna figure out a way to save our club that doesn't involve sausages.' Becky scanned each face. 'So who's with us?'

Every hand shot up in the air except Carly's. Becky grinned. She was so determined to do this, and we all knew that the club meant more to her than anything.

'I've got a few ideas but I wanna hear yours as well.' Becky took a notepad and a pen from the pocket of her jacket.

'Give each new member a free cap?' Sandra suggested, then sneezed so loudly even Flea stopped digging in his ear. Becky scribbled on her pad. Operation Brainstorm was underway.

'Make flyers. Let everyone know what we do and how totally fun Riding Club is.'

'Showbags!'

'Put on an Open Day. Get everyone to make posters and tell all their friends.'

'Organize a merge — you know, Pinebark Ridge and us,' said an Under 10s boy called Justin. The Creekers howled derisively. He may as well have asked us to give up horses altogether. The Ridgers were our mortal Riding Club enemies (except Pree — she couldn't help being a Ridger any more than we could help being Creekers. Besides that, we loved her).

Justin's face was as red as a Trailers' polo shirt. 'Sor-ry! It works in footy.'

'So go play footy,' Carly snapped. It was one of the only times I'd ever agreed with her.

It wasn't long before Becky was shaking her writing hand. 'I've got one more idea.' She nudged me and smiled. 'And this is when I turn the meeting over to Ash.'

'Me?' I gulped. I wasn't the biggest fan of public speaking.

'Yes, you,' Becky muttered through clenched teeth. 'You promised you'd coach us in polocrosse.'

'I never!' I gasped. 'Since when?'

Becky turned on the look, the puppy dog look. 'Please? For me?'

I sighed and covered my face with my hands for a moment. 'I just don't see how this'll make a difference.'

Becky was on her feet in an instant. 'Are you kidding? Once everyone knows just exactly how so so fun polocrosse is we'll be fighting 'em off with our sticks!'

'Might not be the best way to attract new members, Beck.' I sighed again. 'But I'll give it a go. Just remember I'm pretty new to polocrosse myself.'

Becky beamed and settled herself back down on her log. 'No worries!'

I stood up and pulled my mobile phone out of my pocket. Eleven minutes 'til lunch was over. Eleven minutes to convince the Shady Creek riders that a polocrosse team would solve the membership crisis and make our club a riding force to be recognized. 'Well … I … uh.'

'Spit it out, willya?' Flea scratched the top of his head, his eyes fixed on my face.

I cleared my throat. 'Has anyone ever heard of polocrosse?'

There were a few nods and murmurs. Two Under 10s girls raised their hands and waved them frantically.

'It's an unreal horse sport and an Australian one at that! The first polocrosse club was formed right here in 1938 and now it's spread all over the world as far as Zimbabwe and Vanuatu and Canada.'

'The first polocrosse club was formed in Shady Creek?' Flea said, frowning in concentration.

'No, you idiot. Spiller meant Australia.' Carly folded her arms and glared at me. She obviously hadn't quite put the grounding and the Riding Club ban behind her yet.

'The first-ever Polocrosse World Cup was held in Australia in 2003 and we won that one, so all of us should have it in our blood. Twenty-five thousand people came out to watch the matches and over two hundred Australian horses participated.'

'Bits and bridles!' Justin said. 'That's a lot!'

'During polocrosse season there are games on every weekend so Becky's got the right idea. If we could get some teams going we could get new members.' I took a breath. Becky was always the one who could take charge, talk to a group and make people listen. I didn't know if I had that magic in me at all.

One of the hand wavers asked what 'polocrosse' actually was.

'Polo, lacrosse and netball in one, played on horseback.' I smiled at her.

'Cool,' she said, nodding in approval.

I told them as much as I could about the sport in the nine minutes I had left, from the aim of the game to how many players were on a team, to what a field looked like and who was in control. Their eyes were wide and their mouths were open.

'Both boys and girls can play in one team so that's good for us,' I said. 'But there are also teams of three boys and three girls. At the match the boys play the boys and the girls play the girls. And there can be family teams and mixed-age teams. Gary could play, and Flea — you should try to get your mum to join as well. Most of us will only be able to play in Juniors which are Under Sixteens or Sub-Juniors, or Subbies — they're the Under Tens.'

The Under 10s high-fived but the Juniors-to-be eyed each other off. None of them were used to playing with such a big mix of ages. I'd done it at Linley and it had been amazing. I'd been accepted by and learned heaps from the older girls. Carly looked uncomfortable. She knew there was no chance she could order older riders around and not end up with a polocrosse ball wedged up her nose.

'Can we ride our own horses?' Flea said. 'I reckon Scud'd be up for it.' Flea gestured towards the corral where the coal-black of coat and of heart, Scud, was scowling and scraping his near foreleg on the ground.

'You can,' I said. The riders breathed out, relieved. 'Scud'd be a great polocrosse horse with all that Western experience. But any horse who is fit to play can play. The best horses are those that aren't too big or too small. Small horses can be wiped out by huge ones, so average is best.' I scanned the corral. 'We're all okay there as well. Quarter Horses, stock horses and Thoroughbreds make really good polocrosse horses. But all breeds play.'

'What do we need?' Sandra asked, just before sneezing into a tissue.

I ticked off on my fingers. 'White joddies or jeans, a white helmet, our club shirts and a stick. Balls help, too.'

'Stick? Like, off a tree?' Justin scrunched up his face, thinking hard.

'A polocrosse stick,' I said, then told them all about the squash racquet–like, loose-netted stick which players use to pick up, carry and throw the thick-skinned rubber ball. 'Our horses will need a few things, too. Leg bandages, bell boots and whips if you need them. And you'll all have to learn how to tie up their tails.'

'What do we win?' an Under 10s (Subby) girl called out. Her friends chattered at once.

'You can win trophies or ribbons, or sometimes even prizes you can use, like things for your horse.' I felt comfortable now in front of the group. 'But the best thing is the fun! Polocrosse is fast and funky — once you play it you'll be hooked. Even watching it gets you polocrosse mad. Look at Becky!'

Becky crossed her eyes and stuck out her tongue and the Subbies giggled. 'So, we all in?'

The whole club broke out in chatter.

'Anybody out?' Becky stood up and settled her hands on her hips.

'Sounds like a waste of time to me,' Carly sneered. 'I say we just stick to what we know. Mounted games and gymkhanas and stuff. Why start all over again?'

'If you like mounted games you'll love polocrosse,' I said. 'And if the club keeps losing members the way it has, you might not be able to do any of that stuff anyway.'

'But all that gear'll cost heaps of money,' a Subby girl said. 'I don't reckon my mum can afford it.'

'We'll fundraise,' I said. 'Subsidize everything.'

'Cool!'

'So, we're all in?' Becky said again. The eagerness in her eyes was enough to convince those who were unsure. Every hand shot straight up. Carly stared at Flea, whose arm was as straight as a polocrosse goalpost, and finally held her hand up at shoulder height, protesting to the last.

'Oi, you lot!' Twenty-seven heads twisted around. Gary Cho was standing by the corral pointing at his watch. 'Time for games!'

The Shady Creek riders scrambled to their feet and to their horses. I felt good, that for the first time ever we were one club, united. Becky and I jogged across the paddock, past the cross-country course and towards the corral where Cassata and Charlie were resting side by side.

'Tack race?' I said.

Becky gave me a high-five. 'You betcha!'

We were tacked up within a few minutes and ready to ride. I missed Honey so much and I wanted to be riding her here, at home, at Shady Creek Riding Club. But I'd told Becky and myself over and over that floating her up and down every few weeks wasn't going to do her any good. My head kept telling me that she'd be fed and watered and her rug would be checked and that she'd have Rose to keep her company. But my heart was telling me very different things.

'Good to have you back, Ash,' Becky said as we mounted. She gave me a smile. I knew she wanted me to be the person I used to be, to be the totally horse-mad Ashleigh Miller who lived, breathed, slept and loved all things horsy.

'Good to be back.' I settled into Cassata's saddle and stretched my legs, then gathered my reins.

We rode together towards the starting line. Gary had planned an afternoon of easy mounted games like the three-legged sack race. We were going to tackle this one in pairs. Beck and I and two other pairs of riders had to ride from the starting line to a flag that Gary had driven into the ground, with one of us carrying an empty sack. We then had to dismount, stick one leg in the sack each and lead our horses back to the starting line. Sounded like awesome fun!

'We'll need to get busy with ideas,' I said to Beck as Gary passed out the sacks. He beamed up at me from underneath his tattered blue Shady Creek Riding Club cap. A whistle was slung around his neck.

'For what?' Becky tucked the sack into the seat of her joddies.

'Fundraising!' I said, nudging Cassata into place beside Charlie. The Under 10s were going out first so we had a few moments to talk strategy. 'We need gear. Do you know how much sticks cost?'

Becky gave me a blank look. 'Um, no.'

'A good one is pricey.' I threaded my reins into place, watching the Under 10s carefully. The wavy-hand girls were coming first. Oops. Last. Those sacks could get your feet tangled! 'We can get away with three sticks per team and just share them. A spare'd be good. But it'd be better if we had one each. At one carnival a team can play between four and six games. What'll we do then?'

Becky looked a bit pale. 'I didn't know they were expensive.'

'It's your most valuable piece of gear.' Gary blew the whistle and the Under 14s moved forward — it was our turn! I leaned a little forward in the saddle and gathered my reins. I felt bubbly in my tummy. This was my first mounted game since I'd been back on a horse. Could I still do it?

I looked down the line at our competition. Carly and Flea had paired up (no surprises there) and

Sandra was riding with an Under 12 girl called Jayne. Carly and Flea had their heads together.

'Remember to try to ride together,' Becky hissed. 'And arms around waists on the way back. Should keep us in time.'

I smiled. 'Yes, boss.'

Gary raised the whistle to his lips and blew and the Under 14s burst from the starting line in a flurry of legs and tails. I felt Cassata stretch out underneath me. She was older than Honey and nowhere near as fast, but she was willing and tried her best. Jenna had had her first-ever riding lesson on Cassata and I trusted the Appy mare with the Quarter Horse body with my life. I sank into the saddle and called on every riding instinct I had. I could handle not winning this. All I wanted was to finish.

'Go, Ash!' Becky shrieked and I realized I'd fallen behind by a whole horse length. I squeezed my legs against Cassata's sides and gave her her head. There wasn't much further to go. Becky was at the flag, all legs in the air as she dismounted, but there was nothing she could do until I was on the ground as well, one of my legs in the sack.

I shook my feet free of the stirrups and pulled Cassata up then scrambled from the saddle and pulled Cassata's reins over her head, grabbing her reins under her chin in my left hand. I was so used to leading with my right, but Beck had got in first.

'C'mon, c'mon!' Becky yelled as Flea and Carly began tripping their way back to the starting line. Beck's left leg was already in the sack. She held it open for me and I shoved my right foot inside.

Becky wrapped her left arm around my waist and I wrapped my right around hers.

'On the count of three!' she cried. 'Outside leg first. One, two, three!'

We took our first few steps, our horses following behind. Sandra was having a sneezing fit and had fallen out of her sack, but Flea and Carly were ahead.

'Count with me.' Becky squeezed my middle. 'One, two. One, two.'

We walked, then jogged side by side — one, two, one, two. Our horses trotted alongside. Before long we'd caught up to Flea and Carly.

The Shady Creek riders were cheering. Most of them were either afraid of or annoyed by Carly and Flea and weren't really trying to hide their support for us.

'Becky, Becky, Becky, Oi, Oi, Oi!' they chanted. 'Go, Ash!'

We jogged faster. It wasn't easy in that sack, especially dragging Cassata (who looked at us with patient dark eyes, wondering what all the fuss was about) towards the finish line, but we finally did it. We made it over the finish line first by a hair. I grabbed Becky around her neck and we jumped up and down, 'whoo-hooing' at the top of our lungs, as high as draft horses!

Someone grabbed my arm. 'Just go back where you came from.'

I tutted, shaking my head at Carly. 'Moving on is very important for your emotional and spiritual growth. All these negative feelings will end up eating you up inside and the only person who's gonna suffer is you.'

I grabbed Carly's hand with mine and pumped it. Carly was staring at me, her mouth hanging open like an 'O'.

'I'm saying this to you because I wanna help you, Carly. If there's anything I can do, just call.'

Becky's hand was clamped over her mouth. She took a huge breath and gulped, choking down laughter as we staggered away with our horses in tow leaving Carly staring after us, still stunned, still open-mouthed. 'You're insane!'

'For a while anyway,' I said, pushing my foot into my stirrup. I bounced, sprang and sat. 'But you know what, Beck? That accident and all that bad stuff that went along with it … it taught me heaps.'

Becky mounted and settled into her saddle. 'Such as what?'

'Such as life's too short to be angry mad. It's such a waste of time. I say, be horse mad instead!' I grinned at her from underneath my riding helmet. I was back and I felt on top of the world.

eleven

Stable Talk

'So what did you guys decide to do?' Emily looked over her glasses at me and folded a pancake in half, then in half again. I watched in horror as she crammed the whole thing in her mouth.

'Em, that's so gross!' I sliced away a neat chunk of pancake with my knife and fork and waved it at Emily. 'This is the way it should be done.'

Em held her hand up in the 'stop' sign while she chewed. She swallowed and took a long drink of milk from her glass. 'You gotta get it while the going's good around this place. Don't forget I've got a big brother and sister at home. I'm used to having to fight for food! You still haven't answered me, by the way.'

'An Open Day.' I took a bite of pancake and grinned, sticky bits stuck all over my teeth. It was so good, all sweet and warm.

Em rolled her eyes. 'And you reckon I'm gross! What kind of Open Day?'

'It's gonna be so cool,' I gushed. 'We're having a cake stall and a white elephant stall and riding demonstrations and pony rides!'

'What about food?'

'I just said cake stall.' I frowned.

'You'll need more than that. Just leave it to me.' Em stacked her plate with another four pancakes.

'What can you do from here?' I said. Then it hit me. 'Oh wow, oh wow!'

'What?'

'Don't you see? It's on an exeat weekend — you could come home with me! It's just what we talked about. It's perfect!' I was so excited I wanted to twirl pancakes on my fingertips.

'Yes!' Emily's glasses steamed up instantly.

It all ran through my head. There was so much to do and so not enough time.

'What're you doing today?' Em said, polishing off another pancake. I was amazed and fascinated all at once. Where did she put it all?

'The usual,' I said, shrugging. 'English, Music, Art … Horsemanship!'

'No wonder you look like the horse that got the hay.' Em quickly gobbled down her last two pancakes and washed them down with a second glass of milk. We put our dirty dishes on the trolley and rushed out of the dining room. It was time for another day at Linley to begin.

'More Natural Horsemanship — sound like fun?'

'Yes!' Year Seven Horsemanship chorused. We were standing in a group by one of the round yards. I couldn't believe I'd spent seven whole school years not at Linley.

Demi was inside the round yard with a stack of bound booklets in one hand and Cougar's lead rope in the other. She passed the booklets to Nina, who was standing at the front. Nina took one, passed the rest on and pored over hers immediately.

'We've talked about horses as social herd animals whose main concern is survival. We've also talked about horse communication and body language and what Natural Horsemanship actually means. Any questions about anything we've learned so far?' Demi watched us expectantly, but we were silent.

Personally, I had a tonne of questions but I didn't want to look silly — or like a know-all. A booklet entitled *What Is Natural Horsemanship?* was passed to me and I opened it eagerly. I couldn't wait to read it.

'Today we're gonna talk more about horse communication.' Demi's knee began to jiggle. I could tell she was really worked up about what she wanted us to learn. 'It's just so critical to know and read the body language of your horse. They're speaking to you all the time, telling you how they feel and think and what they want. It's up to you to listen. Remember that you're choosing to enter their world, it's not the other way around.

'Who here thinks they're a pretty good rider?' Demi said. She waited for a show of hands.

It was slow, but it came. After a minute almost every girl had her hand in the air, including me.

'That's great news,' Demi said. 'But out there in horse land it counts for only a fraction of your skills. If you're going to be complete horsewomen there's so much more to learn. We're only just beginning on what I hope will be a long journey of discovery and understanding.'

Demi removed Cougar's halter and turned to face him. 'What we'd love for you to develop with your horse is a relationship of trust. This takes time. You have to let the horse guide you and remember that he's the teacher and you are the student. Above all else you have to love, respect and understand your horse.

'Anyone can be a horse whisperer,' Demi continued, stroking Cougar's face. 'There's no magic involved. It's not something you have to be born with. You just need to take the time to learn the language that your horse is speaking and when you do, you'll be amazed just how hard he'll try to please you.'

Demi stood beside Cougar and pawed her foot on the ground. Once. Twice. Cougar pawed the ground as well. Once. Twice. We all gasped.

Demi stood in front of Cougar, looking into his eyes, then walked in a circle around his rump. He watched her, then turned a perfect pivot, following her. She stood in front of him again and raised her arm, like she was pointing. Cougar reversed, taking a few steps backwards until Demi lowered her arm and he halted. Demi made the 'come here' gesture with her hand and Cougar walked towards her. He got a nice rub and a cuddle as a reward when he reached her. Demi stuck both her arms out and

Cougar walked away. She swung one arm around and he began to circle her, like he was being lunged. Except there was no lunge line, no halter and no lunging whip. There was just Cougar and Demi and his trust in her was clear to see. Demi bowed and Cougar returned to her, and he was rewarded again with a rub and a cuddle.

'What do you all think?' Demi asked.

We were speechless, the whole class. I couldn't think of a thing to say except, 'Wow.'

'What just happened here isn't magic and there were no tricks,' Demi said. 'What you saw was trust, communication and a good relationship. It doesn't happen in a lesson or in a week. It takes as long as the horse needs and requires patience.'

I nodded, praying hard to the horse gods that I would be able to store every word she said somewhere in my brain.

'What do we have to do to make our horses do that?' Sandy said with her hand in the air.

'You can't make your horse do that,' Demi said. 'Well, I guess you could make him. But we want him to do things because he wants to, not because he's being made to. Do you understand?'

Sandy nodded. 'Yes.'

'The first thing is trust. I want Cougar to trust me. I want to have his confidence.' Demi rubbed Cougar's neck. 'As a young rider I had to learn that if I tried to dominate my horse with fear or pain, he would most likely run. I had to allow him to choose to follow me as his leader.'

'But how do we do that?' I said. I was practically bursting I was so desperate to know.

'It all begins when a horse is started — that's what Natural Horsemanship trainers call "breaking in" now. They don't get a horse saddled and ridden for the first time by breaking their spirit, hurting them or frightening them. They invite the horse into a friendship with them, then, once the horse trusts them, they introduce a saddle and a rider in a gentle way. The horse knows that they're not going to be hurt so they accept the human into their world much more readily.'

Demi haltered Cougar and led him from the round yard. Joe was waiting nearby. He took Cougar and handed Demi the lead rope of a young horse I'd never seen before.

'This is Sophie,' Demi said. She held firmly to the bay filly's long, coiled-up lead rope. The filly tugged against the rope. She was obviously not at all happy about being haltered. 'She's not yet been started and is only just beginning on a halter and lead rope.'

Demi unclipped the lead rope and Sophie sprang away from her. 'I've told you guys before that horses are prey animals, flight animals. If they sense danger, they'll run. Sophie's instincts have told her to run away from me. What I want to do is get her trust.'

Sophie trotted around and around the round yard, looking for an exit. Joe stood close by, at the gate. His eyes were fixed on Sophie.

'I want her to run from me now, girls.' Demi waved her arms out wide and made loud kissing noises. Sophie trotted faster, to the right. Demi followed her then let out the lead rope and gently flicked the end with no clip behind Sophie's rump. Sophie broke into a canter. 'If the rope hits her it won't hurt her, guys. The last thing I want to do is give her any pain. I want her to come to me because she wants to.'

Demi approached Sophie quickly and the filly stopped cantering. Demi raised her arms again, like she was shooing Sophie away, and made the kissing noise and flicked the lead rope out once more. Sophie took off again, this time in the opposite direction, her head straight, not looking at Demi.

'I want her to use both directions in the round yard. I want her to really try to get out of here and away from me. That means that when she comes to me, if she comes to me, it's because she's not wanting to escape from me but to be *with* me.'

Sophie cantered around and around, Demi following her, raising her arms, flicking and talking. Demi's voice was calm and consistent. 'I'm going to stop using the rope now. Let's see what happens.'

Sophie cantered another lap or two then slowed to a trot. 'Watch her, Year Seven, watch for her body language. She's talking to me. Wow — what did you just notice?'

Sandy wiggled her hand. 'She just looked at you!'

Demi's face didn't change but I could see in her eyes that she was pleased. 'Correct. She just looked at me. She's starting a conversation with me. Now what do you see? Look hard, learn to speak her language.'

I watched the filly carefully. She looked at Demi again and Demi made the shoo movement. This time I understood why. Demi wanted Sophie to accept her as the leader of her herd. I kept watching. The whole class was silent. That's when I noticed.

'Her ear!' I said. 'It's her ear. The one closest to you.'

'Right, Ashleigh,' Demi said. Sophie kept trotting, around and around. Apart from that one moment of changing direction, she hadn't stopped moving. 'Her ear is pointed towards me. That's another sign that she's speaking to me. I'm keeping eye contact with her, and I'm facing her, telling her that I'm the leader of the herd. Did you see that, everyone? That's so important, what she just did.'

I strained to see. What had Sophie done that had got Demi so excited?

'She's done it again. She's licking and chewing. It's her way of telling me she trusts me. Now we'll wait and see if she … yes, she's just done it!'

Sophie was still trotting, Demi following after her. The filly was still licking and chewing. But now her head was down, her nose drooped so low it was almost scraping the ground of the round yard. I'd never seen anything like this ever, in all my horsy life.

'Good girl,' Demi said. 'Very good girl. You see how her nose is low to the ground, Year Seven? That's a precious moment. Sophie's telling me she accepts me.'

Sophie halted and turned towards Demi, but Demi shooed her again and the filly resumed trotting. She kept licking and chewing though. I understood. At last I understood. Demi needed Sophie to absolutely know that she was the leader, that she could be trusted. And Demi would know when the right moment was to invite her in.

'Now watch what I do,' Demi said. 'I'm going to hand over to Sophie. I'm going to drop my eyes and turn my back. I'm making the choice hers now. It's up to her now, whether or not she'll keep running or come to me.'

As soon as Demi turned her back Sophie stopped running. Demi stood still. Sophie dropped her head again and took a tentative step towards Demi. Then another. And another.

The bay filly, who'd run so wildly from Demi just thirty minutes earlier, took three more steps and touched her nose to Demi's back.

'She's done it, guys,' Demi said. 'She's chosen to be with me.'

Demi turned slowly and reached her hand out to Sophie. The filly winced a little, but didn't run. Demi rubbed Sophie's face. 'Good girl, good girl.'

I wanted to cry, to clap, to cheer — I was so amazed and so changed. There was a language and I could learn it. I wanted to try it immediately but I knew I had so much more to learn.

Demi rubbed Sophie's face then held her halter. 'Now I'm going to bring her in closer to me; in to my chest. I'm still not looking into her eyes. That's what predators do. That tells her to run. I'm keeping my eyes low and just rubbing her and letting her in. Good girl.'

Demi let Sophie stay with her for a few moments. The filly was relaxed and happy. I could see that she trusted Demi already. I wondered if she had the same trust with Lightning and if I could … no, I should never, ever try it.

'Now I'm going to walk away from her.' Demi turned her back again and took a few steps. Sophie followed immediately. 'Notice how Sophie has followed me of her own accord. I haven't clipped a lead rope on her and dragged her. She follows me because she wants to.'

Demi walked in a circle and Sophie followed. She turned right then left and the filly followed her. 'Good, good girl. There's still a heap of work to do here, Year Seven. But we've been very privileged today to see this horse accept a human into her world.'

Demi stood still and Sophie stood facing her. They were a team now. I knew that Sophie's lesson would continue long after ours had ended.

Demi set our homework — to read the first chapter of the booklet and write a reflection on the lesson. I couldn't wait to get started. I knew right then that the way I saw horses, the way I thought about them and the way I related to them would never ever be the same. I knew that I had to learn more and that Sophie was the best teacher I'd ever had.

'I'm going to leave you with a quote from one of the best — Tom Dorrance: "A good trainer can hear a horse speak to him. A great trainer can hear him whisper."'

I would never forget those words. I'd never forget that lesson. I was never going to be the same.

twelve

Truth or Claire

'Guess what?' Claire Carlson was at her desk, I was at mine. I had a tonne of homework to do and no time to waste on a conversation with her.

'You're a jerk and I'm not?' I snapped. She'd been especially annoying since our accidental path-crossing at Rosie's office, subjecting me to thrice-daily room spraying and dizzying swings between deathly silences and crazy rants about the evils of horses. It was like she was trying even harder than usual to keep me at bay.

'No.' Claire laughed. Her bushy hair bounced around her face. 'You're so funny, Ashleigh.'

'Grumph,' I muttered. I didn't want her to think for even a minute that I'd actually spent time worrying about her, wondering what her story was, feeling guilty about not being the best of roommates.

'Did you hear the news?' Claire was pushing it. There was obviously something she was dying to tell me.

'No,' I snapped. 'But I did hear myself telling you not to go anywhere near my side of the room with your stupid spray, so keep your disinfectant to yourself. My desk smells like a hospital.'

'Better than how it smelled before. What do you do? Wipe your pooey boots all over the floor?' Claire shuddered.

We were so totally utterly incompatible. I'd often wondered what Linley were thinking when they decided the horse maddest kid in the school could share a room with the biggest horsephobe ever born. They must have been off their haystacks!

'I do actually,' I said. I was starting to enjoy myself. There was often nothing better after a long hard day at boarding school than a nice juicy fight with Claire. At the very least it gave me a break from my homework. 'Right after I wipe them on your desk.'

Claire went pale and reached for her antibacterial wipes. 'You did not. Did you?'

'Maybe I did, maybe I didn't. I guess you'll never know.' I flipped open my poetry book and sighed. 'Can you give me an example of a metaphor?'

'Yes,' Claire barked, rubbing a stinky wipe all over her desk. 'You are as stupid as a baboon!'

I gave her a look. 'That's a simile. I said *metaphor*.'

Claire threw her used wipe in the bin then pulled another from the box, wiping it over her hands. 'Here's a metaphor for you: horses suck.'

I shook my head and re-read the definition in the book. 'I don't think you're even close. And they don't suck, by the way. Not after weaning, anyway. Though I guess when they drink they're sucking. I've never seen a horse lap like a dog, so maybe you're right, after all. Hey!' I smiled brightly at her. 'You know more about horses than you're letting on.'

'I'll tell you one thing I know about horses,' she said, twisting her bushy brown hair into a ponytail. 'They ain't gonna be here much longer.'

I snapped my book shut. Now she had my attention. 'What do you mean?'

Claire beamed. The only time I ever saw her truly happy was when she was tormenting me. 'Mum's organized another Parents' Association meeting.

There are so many more parents on our side since you were stupid enough to fall off that dumb horse, that the School Board approved it. We really should thank you for everything you've done to help our cause. Wait!' Claire closed her eyes and rubbed her temples in slow circles. 'I have a vision. I can see the future. I can see empty stables being bulldozed!'

'You're insane,' I said, stacking my books in a shaky pile. What Rosie had said to me about stories and everyone having one made sense, but I was in no mood to bother digging for Claire's secret past. 'Certifiably insane.'

'That's a big word,' Claire scoffed. 'Where'd you learn that?'

I was too stressed to bite back. I pushed my chair back and pulled my shoes on over my fluffy purple bedsocks. It was time to act.

'Where're you going?' Claire watched me carefully with wide eyes.

'Far away from you,' I said. With that I stormed from the room, slamming the door as hard as I could, leaving Claire and her speech about not leaving our desks during homework hour behind me. I couldn't have given a hoof trimming about door slamming and homework rules. I wanted out.

I jogged down the hallway and up the stairs then ran until I found Emily's room. I knew we weren't supposed to be banging on our best friends' doors between six and seven, Monday to Thursday nights, but this was an emergency!

Em opened the door. She was wearing a dressing gown with a teddy bear print all over it. Her eyes were all wide, the way they get when she's so deep in Mathsworld that you need an air horn and an electric cattle prod to get any sense out of her.

'Whassup?' she said, swinging her door open wide. It was just as I suspected — Maths books, extra paper for working out mathematical problems and a calculator. She was studying so hard lately. If anyone understood doing everything in their power in order to sit in the saddle, I did.

I barged inside and flopped down on her bed. I liked Em's room so much more than mine. It was a whole floor up so it had a better view. It was warm because she didn't cohabitate with a fruitcake who believed that cold rooms were healthier to live in as germs couldn't grow as fast. It had posters of horses and singers and movie stars and photos of her and me and Ricki on the walls. Em had snacks hidden all over the place and could always spring a party at short notice. Her roommate, Lucy, was usually in the library. And best of all there was no Claire.

'It's Claire!' I whined. 'She's soooo annoying and you know what? She's organized another horse haters meeting.'

'What!' Em's glasses fogged up at once. She was well and truly back from Mathsworld. 'For when?'

'Oh no, I forgot to ask. I was so mad I just took off.' I covered my face with my hands. My chest squeezed and squeezed and my tummy tumbled. It was like the tingles all over again and I hated it.

'She can't win, you know,' Em said. 'It's not like every parent agrees with her mum. Just as many people want the riding program to stay open at Linley.'

'But don't you see?' I wailed. 'It's because of me!' I told Em everything Claire had said about my accident. 'That's the last thing I wanted. If only I hadn't listened to that creep India. None of this would've happened.'

'It probably would.' Em was thoughtful. 'There's no way of knowing for sure. Best thing is to work as hard as we can against them.'

I nodded and sighed. She was right and I knew it. It was so good to have her as a friend. She was a thinker; clear-headed and calm just when I needed her to be. And she'd never once said, 'I told you so.'

'We need to do some digging, I think.'

I looked out of the window. 'Now?'

Em rolled her eyes. 'No. Some figuring out, you dope.'

I shook my head and held up both hands in the 'stop' sign. 'No Maths. No way.'

Em wailed, then tugged at my hand and dragged me to her desk, pushing me down on Lucy's chair which was next to hers. Em jiggled the mouse on her sleek white laptop, logged on to the Internet and typed 'Carlson' in the search bar.

'What are you doing?' I said.

'Something we should have done a long time ago.'

Em's laptop buzzed and tut-tutted and produced a long list of options with '*Did you mean Johnny Carson*' at the top. 'Who's he?'

'Refine your search. Type in "Carlson Wallaby Hill". I'm sure Claire has a house there.' I peeked over Em's shoulder and watched as she tapped on the keys.

'Oh no,' Em murmured. 'Ash, read this.'

'*Teenage boy dies in horse riding accident.* You'd better click on it.' I swallowed hard. The article opened and I flicked my eyes over it. 'I can't believe it.'

'Claire had a brother called Cameron.' Em stared at the screen. Her fingers were limp on the mouse. 'He was only fourteen when he died.'

'But when? How?' I was in shock. I'd lived with Claire for months and never known. Nobody had ever told me. How could they not have told me?

Em pointed at a sentence. '*Severe internal injuries.* The horse spooked while Cameron was riding him on the family property and he fell.' Em sucked in her breath. 'It was two years ago. Hope my mum never hears about this. I'm surprised Murky hasn't blabbed.'

'Wonder what happened to the horse?' I felt weak. Poor Cameron. Poor Claire. Poor President Carlson. No wonder she had issues with horses. I pushed my seat back and got up, then staggered to Em's bed and collapsed on top of it, face down.

'So, whadda we do about this?' Em sat next to me on the bed.

I flipped over onto my back and stared up at the ceiling. 'I don't know,' I said.

Claire had had a brother. President Carlson had had a son. I thought hard. How would I feel if it were me? How would I feel if it had been *my* brother? How would my mum feel? She'd probably hate horses too. In that moment I couldn't have blamed Claire one bit for hating horses. In that moment my heart ached for Claire. No wonder she boarded at Linley. There were no memories of Cameron here. She didn't have to walk past his room or see his photos on the wall or look out across the property knowing that he'd died right there. No wonder she couldn't stand me. I stood for everything she hated, everything she feared. No wonder she didn't want to let me in. I thought about what I'd said to her outside Rosie's office, about her having an issue with horses, and felt sick. Why had they roomed me with her? I sighed. 'D'you reckon Ricki knows about this?'

Em whacked my shoulder and I wriggled over. She flopped down beside me.

'Maybe.'

'India must know and Demi and Maryanne. How could they have been here for years and not know? All the teachers would know and so would Rosie!' I was getting madder by the minute. 'No wonder Mrs Freeman has been foal-footing around President Carlson!'

'You think so?'

'For sure!' I was close to spitting. 'Why else would she be letting her have all these meetings?'

Thoughts were racing around and around my head but the right words weren't coming out. What I wanted to say was that I'd learned something amazing. I'd learned to see things from Claire's point of view, even from President Carlson's. I wanted to say that mine wasn't the only way of thinking, just like Rosie had said. That she was so right — that everyone had a story, and that their story did shape who they were and how they felt and behaved. I wanted to say that I understood this other person more than I had ever understood any other person before. But that didn't mean I was going to just stand by and watch while the horses and dreams of Linley Heights School were ripped away.

'Natural Horsemanship,' Demi began. I tuned out in her class for the first time. There was so much to plan and so much to say at the meeting and I knew the one place I could get it done was in Horsemanship. At the very least I'd be surrounded by like-minded horse maniacs whose equi-vibes would inspire me to think of as many reasons as I could for why the riding program should stay. I took the lid off my pen, slid my notepad under my workbook and began to write a list. Demi's name appeared next to number one. Linley was her home. It was where she'd gone to school and where she worked and where she kept her horses. Her sister, Maryanne, polocrosse captain, was there as well. Their lives would be affected.

Demi talked and girls read aloud and the electronic whiteboard was on and the lesson seemed great from the outside. But I was lost in my list. By the end of the lesson I'd come up with a page full of reasons. Em, Ricki and I had agreed to combine lists at the end of the day.

'I need a quote,' I said as India shoved past me at the end of the class. My pen was ready. I'd scribble it down and use it in our campaign. After all, it couldn't just be us three. We needed as many horsy voices as possible, even if one of them belonged to my nemeses.

'I'll give you a quote. Definition of Ashleigh …' she started, then continued with a lot of words that my gran would have said needed to be scrubbed from her mouth with antibacterial soap.

'I'm serious,' I said.

India looked stunned by my failure to understand. 'You think I'm not?'

She showed me how flexible one of her fingers could be and bounced away. I followed her. 'But you love horses, remember!'

'Nina?' I said as she hurried past. 'A quote for the meeting?'

Nina gladly obliged and grabbed three of her friends. It wasn't long before I had thirty-eight quotes from students in favour of the riding program.

'Ah-hem.'

I spun around, pen and notepad in hand. Mrs Wright loomed over me. Her eyes were a little bloodshot and one of her eyebrows was twitching. Perhaps it was stress.

'What are you doing? Your History homework, I hope.'

I shook my head. 'Horse haters … meeting … list … quotes.'

'What was that? Moats?' Mrs Wright's eyes were narrow and her lips were thin. 'But we're currently studying Ancient Rome. Aqueducts, yes. Moats, definitely not!'

I was crumbling like a two-thousand-year-old monument. I tried to explain. This time she listened.

'May I give you a quote?'

I hung my head and held my pen, ready to write down the date, time and place of my next detention.

'Horses are what make Linley Heights School truly unique. To lose them would be to lose part of our identity. As a teacher I have often seen our girls' love of and enthusiasm for horses and riding flow on to other aspects of school life like History and debating. Mrs Monique Wright, Humanities.' Mrs Wright gave me a small smile. 'Satisfactory?'

I gaped at her. 'Yes, Mrs Wright. Thank you.'

Mrs Wright waved her hand at me dismissively and walked down the corridor, her heeled shoes click–clacking as she went. It was time to contact the school chaplain. I had just been witness to a miracle!

thirteen

Tripping the Funkhana Fantastic

'Rick, you look awesome!'

I stood back and admired my handiwork.

Ricki Samuels, otherwise known as Ricki the Remarkable, magician and best friend extraordinaire, was standing before Em and me in Honey's stall in a Linley polo shirt, riding boots, a pair of dark navy Linley joddies and a black riding helmet. Her wild curls had been tamed into two long braids that tumbled down her back. I'd never known I could do hair. All I'd had to do was imagine her head was a tail and the rest had been magic.

'Say it again, and again!' Ricki twirled like a

ballerina and collapsed on a bale of hay, giggling.

'This your first show?' Emily asked. I could tell she was a little — well — jealous. It was hard to be horse mad and held hostage. She was practically counting down the days until report week. So was I, but for a totally different reason. I was vile at violin, hopeless at History and lousy at Latin. Thank heavens for Horsemanship!

'First show for years and I'm gonna have fun, fun, fun!' Ricki was off her hay bale and doing some sort of dance that involved hopping and a whole lot of elbow flapping.

'That's why they call it a funkhana!' I rubbed away a splodge of mud from my second-best pair of riding boots and tucked my polo shirt into my joddies.

'You gymkhana or funkhana?' Ricki's hopping dance was over. Now she was making weird robot movements. I wondered if I could switch her off by tugging one of her plaits.

'Maybe both,' I said. 'The rules are if you don't win a first or second place in a gymkhana event that you can have a go at the funkhana. Makes it fair for everyone.'

Emily scowled. 'It's not fair. Why can't my mum

just be normal? What've I gotta do? Wear a disguise?'

I gasped and jumped up and down clapping my hands. 'Why didn't I think of this before? Why?'

Ricki stopped, mid-hornpipe. 'Think of what?'

'Em ... disguises! The last event is fancy dress! We could enter you under one of our names — no one would ever know!'

Em made two fists and punched the air. 'Yes!'

'Got any fancy-dress costumes handy?'

Ricki walked like an Egyptian across the stall. 'They don't call me Ricki the Remarkable for nothing!'

Our horses were ready and we were ready: the Linley Heights School monthly funkhana and show was about to begin. It was my first show since the accident and I was so hungry to get into the saddle I could have eaten my stirrups.

Honey looked gorgeous. I was entering her in Breed and Presentation as well as Ridden Classes so it was essential that she look her most beautiful. I'd shampooed her coat, mane and tail the day before, trimmed her bridle path and groomed her until she shone. Then I'd spent an hour twisting her mane into perfect round rosettes. I'd rugged her in a combo, which covered her neck and would (hopefully!) keep her from rubbing or rolling out her rosettes overnight, plaited her tail all the way down to the bottom and released her into the mares' paddock, praying to the horse gods that she'd be as mud, leaves, sticks, grass stain and bite free as possible on show morning.

I'd collected her early from the paddock that morning, picked out the leaves and sticks from her tail, hosed the mud from her feet and resewn two rosettes, then given her an hour-long groom (no grass stains, thank horse gods!). I'd fixed her forelock into a neat rosette, painted her feet, rubbed oil into her chestnuts, chalked her blaze and socks, shaken out her tail (which now looked much fuller thanks to the plait) and braided it to the bottom of her tailbone, then spent another hour and almost an entire can of hairspray on do-it-yourself quarter markings that made her rump look like a shiny, chestnut chessboard. I'd added the finishing touches with a bottle of detangler, which added shine, and rubbed Vaseline around her eyes and mouth. Some riders liked to trim, shave or even pull the whiskers from their horse's muzzles but I left them alone, knowing that she needed them to feel in much the same way that a cat does. Honey's show-do had been finished off with one of the many ribbon browbands I'd made over the last few years. I'd chosen pink and black and she looked awesome!

Mystery was Ricki's for the day and she was the most excited I'd ever seen her, giving a pony in a pellet shop a run for its money! Ricki had ridden before, but she hadn't done a lot of grooming for shows, so she'd worked beside me — that way I could give her lots of tips and pass on tricks. Mystery looked sleek, shiny and ready for anything the funkhana could throw at her. So far Ricki had entered Best Presented Galloway, Funkhana Rider 10 Years and Under 15 Years, Novice Girl Rider 12 Years and Under 15 Years, Horse or Pony with the Cutest Ears and Rider with the Cutest Smile. She'd been working on her smile all morning and, as a finishing touch, was adding the ear wiggle she'd learned as part of her magic act.

Classes were free to enter for Linley girls but three dollars each for everyone else. The last funkhana had been open to Linley girls only and I was very curious to see who else might turn up.

Ricki and I led our horses from the stalls and down to the riding centre. The covered arena was being used for funkhana events and the outdoor arena for gymkhana events. Em followed us, carrying our grooming kits and numbers and wearing a face that could change the weather.

'Em, can you lead Honey?' I said.

Em brightened at once and shoved the grooming kits at me. I was glad to see her happy for the first time that morning.

'Dad!' Ricki shrieked. Honey tossed her head but Mystery didn't bat an eyelid.

I'd met Ricki's dad once before, the night I'd been invited for dinner. Em had been invited as well, but her horrible sister, Mercedes, had got her grounded and she couldn't come.

Ricki's dad had a wide smile, a cowboy hat and a dimple in his left cheek. He had calm green eyes and the hands of a horseman. Ricki handed Em her reins and ran into his arms. Mr Samuels spun her in a circle then held her at arm's length, a huge smile on his tanned face.

'Look at you, kiddo! You're finally looking like a real cowgirl!'

'Actually, I'm not. I look like a real funkhana girl. To look like a cowgirl I need this!' With that Ricki knocked her dad's cowboy hat from his head and balanced it on top of her helmet.

Mr Samuels covered his head with his hands. 'I've got hat hair!'

They laughed together and I felt a terrible twinge of homesickness. I missed my dad. I missed his rotten jokes and his terrible cooking and hearing him argue with Mum over the TV remote. I loved falling asleep in my bed, in my room, just knowing that he was there. I loved the way he loved me and Jase and Mum. He was the best dad in the whole world.

I sneaked a look at Em, hoping I was hiding how rotten I felt inside. I may have been homesick, but all my horsy dreams were laid out at my feet. I watched as my friend gazed at one horse, then another and sighed, her eyes filled with longing, and I understood.

'So, how's the riding, girls?' Mr Samuels settled his cowboy hat back on his head and smiled.

'You remember my dad, don't you?' Ricki hung from her dad's arm and beamed.

'Could be better,' I said wryly. 'It's not the riding really, it's the horse haters.'

The four of us talked and talked. About the meeting and what we had planned, and what we might do if it didn't turn out the way we hoped.

'We're going to work this out, girls. Try not to worry,' Mr Samuels said, then he picked up each of

Mystery's feet.

The gymkhana was about to begin. I wished Ricki luck and left her in her dad's care. He looked like he well and truly knew what he was doing. I had a date with a Led Class and I didn't want to be late.

The Galloways Over 14 Hands High Class was about to start. Joe stood at the gate of the outdoor arena bellowing.

'Galloways Over Fourteen Hands High — Led Galloway, Linley students, Led Mare!'

'That's me!' I yelped. I led Honey towards the ring. It was strange, getting ready for a show class on my own. There had always been someone — Becky, Pree … now I was alone. No Mum, no Dad, no friends. I had no one to prove anything to but me.

Honey seemed to know we were on show. She arched her neck and her tail and seemed to take more graceful steps than usual. I led her into the arena. The judge watched us carefully. My tummy tumbled with nerves. Each horse and handler took turns to walk, then trot around three witches' hats, stand, reverse, turn and stand again.

When it was over, a bay mare was awarded the first-place ribbon, Honey nabbed second and a coal-black mare third. I held tight to my ribbon. Our first ribbon of the day was won and I could relax. It didn't matter what happened now — we had a placing, so we were okay.

Another class — Junior Handler 12 Years and Under 15 Years — but no placing. I could handle that. It happened.

Next it was time for the Ridden Classes — the classes where it really counted. While the Leadline Rider and Novice/Beginner Rider Classes were on I tacked up Honey. We had time for a quick warm-up, then Joe was calling our class.

I led Honey into the outdoor arena for the Girl Rider 10 Years and Under 13 Years Class and mounted. I settled into the saddle and cast an eye over the competition. Most of my riding class were cantering around the arena, warming up. There were a few girls I'd never seen before and I assumed they were from other schools. I joined them on the inside track at a walk, then moved Honey to a trot, then finally a canter in the outside track. She was fit and limber, and by the time Joe bellowed that the class was starting and for all riders to halt and wait for instructions she was warm.

'Riders, walk!' A senior girl called out instructions over the loudspeaker. Music was playing and crowds of riders and spectators watched from the grandstand.

I rode Honey at a walk around the arena. The judge stood in the middle.

'Riders, change direction,' called the senior girl.

I turned Honey on the spot and walked her anti-clockwise.

'Riders, rising trot.'

Honey responded to my signals and trotted. I rode her at a rising trot until the next instruction — sitting trot.

'Riders, canter.'

I squeezed my legs against her middle and Honey stretched out into a canter.

'Riders, change direction at a serpentine.'

The rider closest to the top right-hand corner of the arena turned her horse left and rode diagonally across the arena to the bottom left corner then turned him right. I followed suit, changing direction at a serpentine.

'Riders, halt.'

Honey halted, recognizing the word and listening to my signals. I patted her neck and told her she was a good girl, the best girl ever.

The judge walked around the arena, handing out sixth to first places in reverse order. I was stoked to get a red second-place ribbon. India got a yellow fourth, which stoked me even more. One of the girls from another school came first. She grinned and dismounted, leading her coal-black gelding from the arena and rushing to her parents who looked just as thrilled. I wished for a moment that my parents were here to see me. They were working and they had Jason and they'd called earlier in the morning to wish me luck but it wasn't the same.

The Boy Rider 10 Years and Under 13 Years Class was called and Linley girls giggled and crowded around the arena. I rolled my eyes — knowing that a good dose of Flea, blue eyes or not, would cure them of boy craziness before you could say 'King Creep' — and got ready for my next class.

As second place winners in our Ridden Class, Honey and I were automatically entered in the Champion and Reserve Champion Junior Rider Class. After performing almost the exact same routine we did in the Ridden Class, we won — whoo-hoo! As soon as we'd had our photo taken for the *Linley News*, the school newsletter that went out online on Fridays to all Linley families, we were free to get ready for our next class — Show Hunter Galloway 14,2hh ne 15hh. In other words, all horses between 142 and 150 centimetres tall at the shoulder, regardless of rider, gender or breed, could be entered. I had to change, though. I could get away with the Linley polo and dark navy joddies in other classes, but in hack classes they weren't allowed.

Honey and I jogged back to her stall. The stalls were buzzing with riders and horses and parents and friends. The riders from other schools had hired empty stalls for the day. Stalls or floats on show days were an absolute must.

Once inside the stall, with Honey's reins safely secured, I stashed my ribbons in my change-of-clothes bag, ripped off my boots and navy joddies and wriggled into my beige joddies. I tore off my polo shirt, changed into a long-sleeved white shirt and pulled an elastic-necked navy-blue Linley tie over my head. I slipped into my dark navy Linley hacking jacket, the one I had promised my mum only to wear if I absolutely had to, and settled my black helmet back onto my head.

I grabbed Honey's reins. We only had about five minutes left until the class started.

'Ash!' Em was running down the aisle, dodging horses and riders. She banged into a senior girl who shouted some choice words at her.

'What?' I said. I had four minutes to go. There wouldn't be enough time to lead Honey down to the arena now, so I'd have to ride her.

'It's Lightning.' Em panted for breath. Her glasses were fogged up, the way they always did when she got upset. 'I just heard.'

I was starting to panic. My chest felt tight and my tummy felt sick. I hated the suspense and wanted to shake the news out of her. 'What?'

'They've decided. The Board. They want him to be destroyed.' Em collapsed on an upturned milk crate.

'Are you sure?' I gasped. 'Em, are you sure?'

Em nodded. 'It's true. Ask anyone. Ask Demi if you like.'

'But how do you know?' I cried. I didn't care about the show anymore. I didn't care about anything but Lightning.

'Claire told me,' Em gulped, still panting. 'They decided late last night. Demi knows.'

My heart thumped so hard it hurt my head. 'Is

she okay?'

Em looked into my eyes and shook her head and I slumped down beside her.

Lightning was going to die and it was all my fault.

fourteen

Polo-crossed!

'Welcome back to polocrosse, Ash!' Maryanne James beamed at me from Cavalier's back. Her pure white gelding was the only Camargue at Linley and he was one of the best polocrosse horses anywhere in the district.

I smiled weakly. 'Thanks.'

I could barely look at her. Not only was she polocrosse captain and I'd been out for half of the term, but she was Demi's sister which made her Lightning's aunty. She probably hated me right now as much as Demi did.

I rubbed Mystery's neck. Honey was in training, but still hadn't earned her stripes as a polocrosse horse. Not until she stopped shying at the horn, anyway. Mystery was fresh from her funkhana success. Ricki had won first place in Best Presented Galloway, fourth in Funkhana Rider 10 Years and Under 15 Years, second in Novice Girl Rider 12 Years and Under 15 Years, eighth in Horse or Pony with the Cutest Ears and another first in Rider with the Cutest Smile. She'd proudly told me that the ear wiggle had taken her across the finish line.

'You ready to rock?'

I nodded, confused by her friendliness. 'Yes, but—'

'No buts!' Maryanne said. 'Polocrosse.'

I sighed and followed my team out onto the field for a quick practice and warm-up. I was still new to polocrosse, having only played for one term, and was nervous about playing in case I made a mistake. I hadn't slept well since the news about Lightning and I'd pushed my breakfast away that morning. No matter what I did I couldn't stop thinking about the beautiful stallion and trying to come up with ways to save him.

I shook my head. I had to focus on the game. I had to have a win. A reserve called Jessica Haddad, also from Year Seven, had taken my place while I was injured, and now I had to prove myself fit and reliable or risk losing my position to her completely.

Maryanne had us ride our horses in steady laps around the polocrosse field at a canter. Cleo Anderson, a Year Eight, looked so comfortable on the back of her gelding, Dallas, that somebody should have brought her a fan and a bowl of grapes. The other Year Eight, Sarah De Silva, was so focussed on her mare, Pixie, that it would have taken a bomb going off inside her helmet to get her attention.

The Year Nines, Katie Muir on Caramel and Stephanie Costa on Chops, were cantering in serpentines around the field and India McCray was following suit on her chestnut gelding, Rusty. I had nothing against Rusty — it wasn't his fault his owner was an extreme jerkette — but I hated that India had a chestnut too.

Mystery was as cool as a steel hoof pick in a Snowy Mountains stable. She didn't flinch when Maryanne blasted the air horn to get the horses used to it. She didn't bat an eyelid when Maryanne passed me my stick or when I waved it around as I rode. She practically yawned when the six of us rode past one another, tossing the ball between us. She was a great polocrosse horse, but I couldn't help but wish I was riding Honey instead.

Maryanne called us over. We eyed off the competition. It was a mixed boys and girls team from St Andrew's College, the Catholic co-ed school from Green Valley, the next town. Katie and Stephanie pointed at the boys and smoothed down their eyebrows.

'He's so cute,' Katie said. 'That blond guy. I hope he's not a Year Seven!'

'Settle down!' Maryanne said. 'Don't lose it over some boy. Maybe they sent their best-looking polocrosse player just to put you all off your game. Hey — pay attention!'

Maryanne snapped her fingers and five of the six members of the Linley Juniors turned back to her, their mouths hanging open. There was no putting me off. He could have been Zac Efron for all I cared. All I was interested in was making sure that we scored goals and they didn't.

'We're on a winning streak right now,' Maryanne said, tossing us our bibs. 'It's up to you to keep it up. Katie, Ashleigh and Cleo are up first, then Sarah, India and Steph. Ash, you're Number Two—'

'Finally you see her for what she really is,' India muttered. She'd been pretty quiet since my accident, since being suspended. But I knew she still hated me.

'Keep it off the field,' Maryanne snapped. 'Katie you're Number Three and Cleo, have a go at Number One. Your goal scoring has been totally brilliant lately!'

Cleo glowed with pride. The three of us grouped on the field and waited for the horn.

'Now!' Katie bellowed as the horn blasted and the umpire threw in the ball. St Andrew's pounced and their Number Two scooped it up from the ground, spinning his horse around and galloping towards our goals. He threw the ball to the Number One who crossed the penalty line, charged into the goal-scoring area and fired it into the goal.

The St Andrew's students roared and our heads spun in shock. It had happened in a heartbeat.

'Get with it, Linley!' Maryanne shrieked.

The ball was thrown in again and I stretched up as high as I could, catching it in my net. I swung my net down, ready to tear away, and lost the ball. Cleo dived on it but it was too late. That same boy, the Number One, had it in his net and was gone. The St Andrew's kids screamed again as their second goal was recorded on the scoreboard. It was only two minutes into the first chukka and we were being slaughtered.

The umpire threw the ball in again and both teams swooped. Cleo had it in her net and she spun Dallas on his heels. He burst into a gallop across the field, St Andrew's on his tail. The Number One and Two sandwiched her and she was trapped. She flicked the ball to me. I leaned forward, my stick outstretched, and missed. St Andrew's had it in their net and in our goal in five seconds.

I shook my head — this was like no polocrosse I'd ever played! My first game since the accident and they were wiping the field with us.

The ball was thrown in and again they pounced, but despite the thrashing horsy legs, Katie held the ball in her net.

'Ashleigh!' she bellowed as she galloped away. 'Help!'

I turned Mystery towards her and chased her, cutting off the deadly St Andrew's Number Two. He raised his stick, enraged, and brought it down across Mystery's rump. The whistle blew and the umpire held her racquet just under the net sweeping it down and to the left — St Andrew's had just handed us a free shot at goal for hitting a horse with the racquet and their Number Two was warned. Another strike and he'd be suspended for a week.

Cleo shot for goal and made it. Linley students whooped and cheered. Finally we'd made a mark on the scoreboard. The horn blew again and the chukka was over. Katie, Cleo and I trotted from the field and our second three passed us.

'Nice miss, idiot,' India snarled. 'Thanks for warming up the scholarship for me.'

I scratched my nose with my middle finger. India got the message.

Linley scored nothing in the second chukka but St Andrew's racked up another three goals. We were being thrashed.

'Nice goal, idiot,' I said sweetly as I passed India on my way back out onto the field.

India told me exactly what I could do with my middle finger.

Katie, Cleo and I managed one goal to St Andrew's four goals in the third. By half-time we were exhausted and freaked.

'I don't know what's happening out there,' Maryanne ranted. 'But do something about it. I don't wanna see that team get another ball through our goals!'

Her pep talk didn't work. By the end of the match the score was Linley Juniors five, St Andrew's

Juniors fourteen. We shook their hands, but the six of us scowled as they sang their school song.

'I need counselling!' Cleo said, wide-eyed.

'I need chocolate.' I dismounted, loosened Mystery's girth and collapsed on the grass. We'd never been so badly beaten.

'I need an explanation!' Maryanne was wound up as tight as a brumby on a lunge. She paced as we cooled out our horses. 'What happened out there?'

Stephanie shrugged. 'They were too good for us.'

'Rubbish!' Maryanne barked.

'We weren't focussed,' Sarah said reflectively.

'We don't have Jessica,' India grumbled. 'Why can't we just have her back?'

Maryanne shook her head. 'Training. You all need extra training. And you, Ashleigh, are going to ride your own horse from now on. You got into Linley with Honey and you'll ride her in competition.'

Maryanne marched across the field. I stared after her. Honey was terrified of the horn. What could I do between now and the next match to help her beat her terror and teach her polocrosse?

'You're lucky to still be on this team,' India spat as I led Mystery to the stalls. She needed a groom and a feed.

'I feel lucky,' I said. I'd made up my mind to ignore her. 'And thanks for the warm welcome back. It meant a lot to me.'

'And the scholarship means a lot to me. Enjoy it while it lasts, Ashleigh. I'm not the only girl at this school with their eyes on that prize.' India smirked and shook her long blonde hair loose.

'Hey, India,' I said, smiling as sweetly as I could. 'Gomo.'

'Which means?' India frowned.

I cleared my throat. 'Get over it and move on.' I gave India my best grin and stroked Mystery's nose. 'The scholarship's mine. If they were going to take it away from me they would have taken it by now. You need to find yourself a new cause.'

India's mouth opened and closed a few times but she said nothing.

As I groomed and fed Mystery, I felt so much older than India, so much more mature. And that feeling stayed with me right up until I filled the pockets of her yellow and green Australian National Youth Equestrian Team jacket with sawdust and dipped the sleeves in Rusty's water trough.

fifteen

Creek, Sweet Creek

'I'm so glad to get out of that school.' I sank into the back seat of Mum's car and sighed. My head was full and I was feeling tired. I needed some time out from Linley and everything that went with it. I'd left my uniform, bag and homework on my bed, telling myself I'd deal with it when I had to. In fact, the only piece of Linley I was happy to take away with me was Emily. The further behind we left the huge stone walls and neatly manicured but untouchable-on-pain-of-lunchtime-detention lawns, the faster the stress oozed from my muscles. I hated leaving my Honey horse behind, though.

'I'm with you.' Em smiled at me and yawned. She was exhausted after all that studying. Her mum had given her permission to come home on exeat with me but on the strict condition that she had to complete a whole new chapter of her extension Maths textbook and have it marked by her teacher before we left. That was on top of all the homework that she already had. I was amazed that anyone would want to spend the weekend at my place so badly that they'd willingly go through all that torture. 'What's for dinner?' Em said and yawned again.

'Mummy?' I said in my best *I'm your firstborn and only daughter and I'm so adorable I just know you'll give me whatever I want* voice.

Mum looked at me over her left shoulder sharply. 'You haven't said "Mummy" since the last time Toffee ate Mrs Adams's begonias. That poor woman. Her garden's never been the same since you moved that horse in. No matter how many times we fix the holes he digs under the fence, he insists on getting out and—'

I stretched forward and rubbed her shoulders. 'Nice Mummy.'

Mum slapped at my hands. 'What's wrong with you? I'm trying to drive.'

'What's for dinner?'

Mum clutched her chest with one hand. 'Is that all? Thank goodness. I thought you were about to tell me you wanted to start dating!'

I recoiled. 'Mother — are you serious?'

'You're getting to that age, Ash,' Mum said thoughtfully. 'And you are at high school now.'

'Two things,' I said, counting off on my fingers. 'Number one, I'm only twelve. Number two, I clearly remember you and Dad making me sign a contract when I was about seven that I would always believe in Santa, the Easter Bunny and boy germs. Number three, Linley Heights is a girls school — that usually means no boys and even more usually … no dating!'

'That was three things,' Mum said. 'And your dad wanted to cook for you girls tonight so I left him and Jase to hold the fort.'

Em and I exchanged nervous glances and clasped our hands together, prayer-to-the-horse-gods-style. After weeks and weeks of horrible Linley boarding-school food we needed seriously good tucker.

'How much longer?' Em said, yawning again.

'Only a few minutes and we hit Shady Creek.' I looked out the window. It was dark — daylight saving time was a mere summer memory — and the trees looked black against the silver clouds. It smelled like the bush, like Shady Creek. I couldn't wait to be home. I couldn't wait to see Dad and Jase and Toffee and I was so dying to introduce Emily to Becky and Pree.

It was the weekend of the Shady Creek Riding Club Open Day and I was a little anxious about how much money we could raise for our polocrosse team. There were uniforms, sticks, balls and goalposts to buy, we had to pay to register with the State association and then there were the yearly membership fees on top of that. The more successful the Open Day was, the less money each team member would have to pay to play polocrosse. The more successful the polocrosse, the better Shady Creek Riding Club's chances of survival.

'So why's Dad making dinner?' I thought about some of his more experimental meals and chewed on my thumbnail. My tummy was aching with hunger and I didn't want thumbnail to be the only thing on the menu. 'I thought it was his turn to pick me up.'

'It's fantastic,' Mum said. 'He discovered a pile of my old cookbooks and he's gone troppo. He makes a new recipe every night and writes up weekly menus and sticks them on the fridge. He even reads cookbooks in bed.'

'Wow,' I said.

'Wow is right.' Mum looked in the rear-view mirror and smoothed down her eyebrows. 'We've been eating like royalty, even Jason.'

'Typical,' I grouched. 'Just when I leave home, Dad becomes a gourmet. He needs to get back to work.'

'You need to eat,' Mum said as we drove past the *Welcome to Shady Creek* sign. 'You're getting grumpy.'

In less than five minutes we were in the driveway. In another two Em and I had slipped through the paddock fence and were groping in the darkness for a miniature horse. In the next minute the miniature horse in question had cantered through both our legs and we were lying flat on the wet grass looking up at the moon.

'Toffee's a little different,' I said, hauling Em to her feet. Toffee trotted up to us with his soccer ball in his teeth. He gave it a shake and took off again, throwing in a few pig-roots for good measure. 'What a poser. I think he's trying to impress you, Em.'

'Are all the Shady Creek horses that weird?' Em dusted off her bottom and untangled her glasses from her hair.

'You think that's weird just wait 'til you meet the riders!' I giggled.

'I'm happy to — wait, that is!' Em laughed and hooked her arm through mine.

'Dinner?'

'Now that's something I can't wait for!'

We followed our noses to the kitchen.

'Aren't they feeding you or something?' Mum watched with distaste as Em and I stuffed ourselves. Jason screeched and rubbed chopped-up spaghetti into his high-chair table with both hands. 'What a gorgeous boy! Is gorgeous, gorgeous.'

I rolled my eyes. 'What's so gorgeous about eating like a pig? How about I tip my dinner out onto the table and do a finger painting for you?'

'Wanna see the photos of you at Jason's age rubbing pumpkin on the wall?' Dad took a sip of water from his glass and grinned, waggling his eyebrows. 'And don't be tipping the delectable home-cooked spaghetti bol made from the sweat of my very own brow anywhere except your small intestine!'

Em took a huge bite and chewed with relish. 'Hmm. Thith ith so good!'

'I don't wanna hear about intestines.' I drained my glass of orange juice and wiped my mouth with the back of my hand. 'Ahhh.'

Mum shook her head. 'Disgusting.'

'You'd be doing the same thing if you boarded at Linley,' I said. I topped up Em's glass and refilled mine. 'We're trying to totally stuff ourselves so we won't be hungry at school.'

'I just can't believe the food's that bad,' Dad said, tearing a huge chunk of garlic bread from the loaf. 'On the first day—'

'First schmirst,' I cried, nudging Emily. 'Tell 'em what we had for dinner last night.'

Emily swallowed her mouthful slowly, savouring every morsel. 'Cold, lumpy instant mashed potato with half-cooked frozen carrots, boiled Brussels sprouts and sickening stew.'

Mum and Dad exchanged a look.

'Sickening stew? Which cookbook can I find that in?'

'*Linley Horror's Most Revolting Recipes*,' I said seriously, helping myself to seconds. Em looked at the half-full serving dish of spaghetti and licked her lips. I filled her plate with more food. She gave me a wink and tucked in.

'Make sure you save room for dessert,' Dad said, his face bright. 'I made banana pudding and real vanilla ice cream.'

I stared at him. 'You made ice cream? All by yourself?'

'Your father's very talented,' Mum said, tousling his hair. I thanked the horse gods that my parents had finally realized that *my* hair was a tousle-free zone. 'He's really found his niche in cooking. I haven't been anywhere near the stove for goodness knows how long.'

Dad leaned back in his chair and patted his tummy. 'Never interfere with a man's kitchen, Helen.'

'I'll remember you said that next time you want me to wash up,' I said, eyeing off the huge pile of pots in the sink. By the look of it, he'd used every pot in the house.

'I'll remember you said that next time you stick your hand out for Horse Cents money!' Mum laughed and did something magical to Jason's high-chair table. It slid away smoothly, smeared spaghetti and all. Mum picked Jason up and let him dangle over the blue plastic splat mat for a moment. Spaghetti rained down, landing on the mat with gentle *phuts*. He reached out for Mum and grabbed her lips, tugging at them like they were elastic bands.

'Glad it's you and not me,' I said, sliding back my chair, getting up and collecting the dirty dinner dishes into a shaky, spaghetti-y pile while Mum stripped Jase down to his bare bottom and carried him upstairs.

'I'll second that.' Dad stretched and yawned. 'Who's ready for dessert?'

'That would be us.' I dumped the dishes on the kitchen bench and pulled out a stack of bowls. 'Em, grab some spoons.' I pointed at the cutlery drawer.

'You got it!' Emily was as hungry for dessert as I was.

Two serves of banana pudding and surprisingly delicious ice cream à la Dad later, Em and I wished Dad a good night's sleep and staggered up the stairs to my room. It had been a big day and both of us had made dates with our pillows.

'It's so peaceful here,' Em said sleepily, snuggling into the fold-up bed that was usually only pulled out for Jenna or Beck. 'Compared to school, that is.'

'Wait 'til you meet the Creepketeers on Sunday,' I said, yawning hugely. 'Nothing peaceful about them.'

My eyes felt heavy and sore. I rolled over onto my tummy and breathed in the smell of fresh home-washed sheets. "Night, Em," I murmured.

"Night, Ash."

I was back home, in my room, safe as a butterfly in a cocoon. It was a great place to be.

'Checking in or out?' I hissed at Dad, my eyes firmly fixed on the kissing couple in the lobby.

'Out.' He tapped at the keyboard of the Miller Lodge computer and checked that all the cords were well and truly in the credit card machine.

'I didn't know you had guests,' I whispered.

Dad blushed red as a Shady Trails uniform and shrugged. 'They didn't come out of their room a whole lot.'

'Oh.' I stepped around them cautiously and took a suitcase handle in each hand. 'Can I take these bags for you?'

There was no response.

'Ash, just leave them on the porch, will you?' Dad had started to sweat. I couldn't understand why. They were in love and I thought they were very sweet but all the same I thanked the horse gods that my parents never kissed.

I deposited the suitcases on the front porch fulfilling my Miller Lodge obligations for the day in one easy move. It was time to get onto the real business of this weekend.

'Em?' I hollered.

'Out here!' I followed her voice to Toffee's paddock. She was leaning through the railings rubbing his forelock. Toffee was almost drooling in delight at all the attention. He was leaning to one side and, if he relaxed even more, was in danger of keeling over completely.

'Time to go to Beck's.' I stood beside her and patted Toff's rump. He looked up at me with dark horsy eyes. 'No, you've been fed.'

'He has?' Em said, looking at her watch. 'Since when?'

'Since five o'clock when I got up to feed him. He can't get Mum out of bed before seven but he knows I'm a pushover.'

'Where's his rug?'

'Over there, airing out.' I gestured at the corral. Unlike with Honey, I didn't trust Toffee with his rug any more than I could piggyback him. I was sure that if I left a miniature horse rug anywhere near his teeth I'd come home to find he'd made paper dolls out of it. 'Thought he might like to get a good roll or two in this morning. Weather's pretty mild and he's a furball.'

'So what'd he have for breakfast?' Em asked as we walked down the driveway. It was totally strange walking to Becky's. I'd only ever ridden there.

'A half dipper of white or wheaten chaff, one of green — that's lucerne — chaff and quarter dipper of pony pellets. He gets carrots sliced up in there too.'

'And your mum does all that for you while you're at school?' Em's eyes were wide.

'Yeah,' I said. 'She does.'

'What a great mum.' Em sighed. 'My mum'd never measure out horse feed for me. You're really lucky, Ash.'

'Yeah,' I said. 'I am.'

As we walked down the street, I thought about my mum. She did get up and feed Toffee for me. I'd shown her how to take his rug on and off and she was always playing around with the automatic watering system she'd invented for me. She went horse-hunting whenever Toffee escaped and made artful apologies to the neighbours that almost always kept me out of trouble. She'd promised to check his feet for me at least once a day and she was always coming home with balls that she'd picked up at the second-hand store in town for him. All so that I could go to boarding school and chase my horsy dreams. I was lucky. I was very lucky indeed.

sixteen

Lamington Lessons

'Becky, this is Emily. Em, this is Becky.'

My two friends waved at one another.

'It's great to have you on board,' Beck said as we followed her into the Cho family kitchen. There was no one else at home. Gary and Mrs Cho were at Rebecca's Garden and Rachael was at Shady Trails. If it hadn't been for the Open Day Becky'd be out too, riding of course.

Becky's face crinkled into a huge smile. 'We need as many people as we can get tomorrow.'

'Em knows all about the Open Day and she's totally psyched. Right?'

Em nodded. 'Sure am. Anything I can do, just let me know. My speciality is food, by the way.'

'Great!' Becky handed Em some cardboard and a packet of brightly coloured markers. In a few moments Em was sitting at the kitchen table carefully copying out the foodstall price list. Becky had organized sausages on a roll, lamingtons, cupcakes and lolly bags. Each item was a dollar and fifty cents, except for the sausages which she'd decided to sell for three dollars. She was also selling lamingtons six per packet for five dollars.

'Where're you getting all this stuff?' I eyed the list.

'Julie and Jodie are doing the cupcakes. Their mum bought this huge sack of cupcake mix from the bakery and they told me they were aiming for two hundred.'

Em's face lit up. 'Yum!'

'The Under Tens are making the lolly bags. They have to put twenty lollies in a little freezer bag and tie up the end.' Becky took a breath and smiled. 'And we're doing the lamingtons.'

'Us?' I was shocked.

'Of course, you. Who else is gonna help me?'

'Pree?' I said hopefully.

'Seriously,' Em said, nodding. 'If it's tasting you need I'm your girl. But cooking's not my strong point.'

Becky shook her head. 'Pree's at home making garlic naan, so it's gonna have to be us.'

'But I've never made a lamington in my life!' I protested.

'You're about to get a crash course. I've got everything ready. All you need to do is dip and roll.'

'And the sausages?'

'Our dads. They're both hauling their barbies to Riding Club in the morning.' Becky rubbed at her forehead the way she always did when she was stressed. 'Dad bought the sausages for a good price through his supplier but I have to pay him back out of our profits.'

'You've been busy,' I said.

'You have no idea.' Becky sounded a little flustered.

'I thought we weren't gonna do sausages again?'

Becky's eyes flashed. 'It was all I could organize on my own. What'd you want me to do, plug a pie-warmer into a tree?'

I held up my hands and glanced at Emily who was staring hard at the floor. 'Okay, okay. I was just asking.' I could tell Becky was upset with me. I hadn't been there to help her like I had been before Linley. I felt mean and embarrassed and angry with myself for not thinking harder.

'A little less conversation, a little more child labour, please.' Becky giggled. Em looked relieved and I knew everything would be okay.

'Don't worry, Beck,' I said, rolling up my sleeves so that I could scrub my hands. 'I like sausages.'

'Good, coz you're on barbecue duty at 12 p.m. Right after your pony ride duty.'

'Anything you say, boss!' I saluted my best friend with a wet hand, then we clung to each other, giggling. Em giggled, too.

Becky wriggled into an apron and pulled slabs and slabs of vanilla sponge cake from the fridge.

'How many are we making?' I frowned at the cake and poked it.

'I figured about two hundred as well.'

'Where we gonna put 'em all?' Em said.

Becky smiled. 'In the cool room. We have a huge one at the restaurant. There are advantages to having a Chinese restaurant in the family.'

Becky showed me how to slice the slabs of cake into squares and then set to work on making the chocolate icing, tipping cup after cup of icing sugar and cocoa powder, some water and a few tablespoons of vanilla essence into a bowl. She mixed it all up with a spoon and, when she was done, dipped a teaspoon into the icing and had a taste.

'Perfect,' she said.

I stared at her, open-mouthed. 'I had no idea you could cook. I thought you only spoke horse.'

'Next time you grow up in a family of chefs, just try to get out of it cooking-skills free.' Becky smoothed down her apron. 'Besides, what difference is there between making lammies and making hot bran mashes?'

I thought about that one for a moment. 'Um. I'd say taste and a whole lot of fibre.'

'Ha-ha.' Becky took out a second bowl and emptied a packet of desiccated coconut into it. 'Watch and learn.'

She picked up one of my vanilla sponge squares, dipped it into the chocolate icing then rolled it around in the coconut. It emerged from its coconut experience as a lamington. Becky held it up. 'Ta da!'

Emily and I clapped respectfully.

'Mind if I give it the taste test?' Em said.

'Just don't digest too many of the profits!'

Becky handed the lamington to Em. She took a bite and gave us the thumbs up. Now that we had the official green light it was time to get down and lammie. With me on chocolate roll, Becky on coconut dip and Em on stacking and quality control, our target of two hundred lammies was reached by lunchtime.

'What next?' I said, finishing off my second helping of Chinese-style vegetables with steamed rice.

'You're so lucky to have a restaurant,' Em said, dreamy-eyed. 'That's it, I'm putting myself up for adoption.'

'I don't always get this for lunch, you know.' Becky gathered up our plates and dumped them in the sink. 'Sometimes I have to eat sandwiches at school just like everybody else.'

'Poor thing,' I said, and gave Em a nudge with my elbow.

'You haven't eaten a school sandwich until you've tried a Linley Horror school sandwich!' Em said as she nudged me back.

Becky rolled her eyes. 'Next we're folding pamphlets.' She disappeared down the hallway and came back with an armful of A4-sized paper. There was writing and photos all over the pages. 'I made these myself.'

I picked up a sheet. 'Great job, Beck. Hey, wow, you even put a membership application form on there.'

'If we can get twenty new members out of this I'd be stoked,' Becky said. 'We're gonna raffle off a couple of year-long memberships as well as some other stuff that's been donated.'

'Let's just hope the winners have horses!' I said. 'You want two folds in these?'

Becky nodded and reached for the phone. She made final reminder calls to all the riders who were doing demonstrations and went over her list again and again.

The last pamphlet was folded, the last lamington was packed away in the cool room and the last phone call had been made. It was finally time for Em and me to go. I hugged Becky tight and promised to be at Riding Club by seven the next morning.

'You sure Toffee can do his usual tomorrow?' Becky said, rubbing at her forehead again.

I turned to Emily who was staring at Charlie and turning a pale shade of green. 'Is Toffee in fine soccer form?'

Em nodded. 'For sure. He's playing better than Harry Kewell.'

'Good.' Becky smiled. She looked tired.

'It'll be okay, Beck. I promise everything'll be okay.'

Becky yawned. 'Hope you're right, Ash.'

'Have I ever been wrong? Hang on — don't answer that!'

Becky grimaced. 'Better for you if I don't!'

I dragged Emily down the driveway and Becky closed her front door. We needed dinner, rest and sleep before tomorrow. The Open Day was the most important thing we'd ever done for Riding Club.

That night in bed, I sent my very best prayers up to the horse gods. *Please,* I begged, *please let a thousand people come and spend their money and join up and make Riding Club be safe. For me, but especially for Becky.*

By the time I was done Em was asleep. I rolled over, stretched, tucked my doona under my chin and yawned. Tomorrow would come and with it either profit or loss.

seventeen

Open Day

'Rebecca, you are a legend!' I grinned at my best friend and wrapped an arm tightly around her shoulders.

Priyanka Prasad beamed, her brilliant white teeth flashing in the sunlight. 'Isn't she? I am truly proud and so very humbled to have Rebecca as a friend.'

Becky shoved me hard. 'Since when do you guys call me Rebecca?'

I laughed aloud. 'Since we wanted to see exactly how you'd react.'

'Where's Emily?' Pree stood on her tippy-toes and squinted into the sea of people. 'I can't wait to meet her. Sorry I couldn't make it yesterday. Mum said that if I wanted to volunteer garlic naan for the foodstall I actually had to be present while it was being made.'

'Pony rides. I can't get her off. She's tried out each horse a few times over. I reckon she's spent enough money over there to keep at least half the club in polocrosse for the next five years.'

Pree raised an eyebrow, then wiggled it. I tried it myself but just wound up frowning. 'Horse person?'

'Horse mad!'

'When her backside's all ponyrided-out send her to me and I'll give her a job.' Becky pointed at her clipboard and a very long list. 'I'm not knocking back any volunteers. I need someone to check that the "back of a ute" sale is going okay.'

'Shouldn't that be "car boot sale"?' I said, confused.

Becky sighed. 'There was too much stuff for one car boot and Dad didn't want too many cars driving all over the place and making grooves — no good for the horses. So Sandra's dad offered us his ute.'

'I'd help you out, Beck, but if I'm seen by even a single Ridger I'll be arrested for treason as soon as I cross back over the border!' Pree looked over each shoulder, like she was being watched.

'You're crazy!' I said, shaking my head.

'You still good for that barrel racing demo, Ash? Charlie's ready. I'd do it myself but I'm way too busy.' Becky crossed something off her list.

I looked down at my joddies, riding boots and Shady Creek Riding Club shirt. 'You betcha.'

Pree whacked both of our arms. 'Stop me if you've heard this one. How do you hire a horse? Put a brick under each hoof! D'you get it? A brick — to make him higher!'

The Shady Creek Riding Club Open Day was in full swing — uh — gallop, and everything had gone to plan so far. There was a banner made from an old Rebecca's Garden tablecloth tied to the front fence of the paddock that said *Shady Creek Riding Club Open Day 10 a.m. – 2 p.m. Come in and join the fun!* The foodstalls were set up along the fence as well. Our lamingtons had their own stall and were selling well. Kids were dragging their parents to the lolly stall and choosing lolly bags from one of the Chos' washing baskets. Julie and Jodie had made cupcakes and iced them in blue, pink, chocolate and yellow and decorated them with rainbow sprinkles. Dad had taken the day off from the B and B to help man the barbie and he and Gary were cooking up a sausage and onion storm. Rachael was on board as well, taking orders, buttering rolls and issuing sausage tickets.

Flea's mum had thought of doing a drink stall and she'd filled tub after tub with cans of fizzy drink and bottles of water and covered them with ice. She saw me watching her and waved. I'd often wondered how someone as nice as her could have produced a boy as disgusting as Flea. Jodie and Julie's mum was busy painting faces and selling pony ears that she'd made herself from headbands and coloured felt.

'Better get into it,' Becky said. She took off carrying a megaphone in one hand and her clipboard in the other. Every fifteen minutes or so she introduced the next riding demonstration. It was Flea's turn to wow the crowd with some Western riding.

Flea was annoying and mean but he was an awesome rider, the best Western rider in Shady Creek apart from Gary. Flea's horse, Scud, had a heart as black as his coat but he was an amazing Western horse and could do things I had only dreamed of, like the Sliding Halt and Rollback.

I pushed my way into the crowd of people. Flea was dressed the part in a pair of blue jeans, dark

243

brown Western boots and black leather chaps, a bright blue shirt with silver tassels and a belt with a huge silver buckle. He wore a black Akubra with a smart brown feather in the rim in place of his riding helmet. He loped Scud around the warm-up arena, holding the split reins with his left hand and allowing his right hand to hang down by his side. I could see that he was neck-reining Scud as he loped in gentle circles. Scud kept his head low, so different from the English riding training I'd been doing at Linley.

The crowd was wowed by the seeming effortlessness of Flea's riding. I knew what he was doing, I knew that Flea was talking to Scud with his legs and hands and seat and that Scud was listening and responding. But his leg aids were invisible. His hands seemed still.

Scud halted immediately and reversed, then broke into a jog. The crowd cheered and clapped as his demonstration came to an end. Flea jogged Scud around and out of the arena. As he left I could see little kids with wide eyes, looking up at him like they thought he was a hero, and in a weird way I was kind of proud of him. I shook my head, trying to shake any kind thoughts of Flea from my mind. He was a

Creepketeer. He was King of the Creeps. He was my revolting neighbour and had christened me with my dreaded nickname, Spiller Miller. But then, even after all that, he'd sort of rescued me from Carly that day. I didn't know what to think!

'You ready?' There was a hand on my shoulder. I turned around and smiled at Becky.

'You bet!'

Barrel racing was my first love. As Holly, my very first riding instructor from South Beach Stables, had always said, *Barrel racing is life, the rest is just details!*

I followed Becky to the corral, where Charlie was waiting. Even though he was my best friend's horse, I'd never ridden him. He was well behaved and willing, though, and we both felt sure that he'd be fine. Becky had had the sense to roster one of the Shady Creek riders on to an hour-long corral duty, so that the horses used in the demonstrations were safe.

'May be a good idea to have a bit of a ride first,' Becky said, untying the twine from Charlie's bridle.

I tightened his girth. Becky had left it loose so that he'd be more comfortable. 'How long since he's done any barrel racing?'

Becky picked up Charlie's near foreleg and gave it a stretch. 'A few weeks. We did it at Riding Club.

Pree came along that day and tried it on Jazz.' Becky smiled. 'Poor Jazzy didn't manage to raise more than a walk.'

My heart hurt for a moment. There was so much that I missed out on when I was away at school. I was starting to feel like an outsider once more. Where exactly did I belong? I wasn't a city girl anymore. I wasn't really a Linley girl yet either — I was too new. The one place I really wanted to be home was Shady Creek, but with each trip back I was beginning to feel more like a visitor.

'He's all yours.' Becky handed me her reins. I'd always loved holding them. They were so well looked after — all Becky's gear was, from her hoof pick to her saddle.

Becky stood back and watched as I mounted Charlie. I wondered what she was feeling, thinking. I'd never seen anyone but her riding him. I remembered Mum crying the first time she'd gone out without Jason. It must have been a bit like that.

'Don't worry,' I said, gathering the reins and wriggling around in the saddle. It was different from mine and I was trying to get settled. To Becky, though, I knew it would have felt like home. 'I'll look after him.'

Becky nodded, smiling. 'I know.'

She turned and left the corral then, once she was a safe distance from the horses, raised the megaphone to her mouth and announced that the barrel racing demonstration would begin in the arena in fifteen minutes.

I could see the whole Open Day from the saddle. There were hundreds of people, at least half of them kids — all potential future members of Shady Creek Riding Club. I recognized lots of kids from primary school and plenty more who'd gone on to Shady Creek and Districts High School, just like Becky and Pree. There were boys and girls running around wearing football guernseys in all colours with stripes and sashes on the front and black numbers on the back. Some of them had footballs under their arms. Becky had told me earlier that Flea had organized a friendly match between Shady Creek Riding Club and the Wombats. I was a bit nervous. I'd never kicked a football in my life and from what little of the game I'd seen on TV, I stood a very real chance of being crushed under a pile of bodies in boots if I so much as touched the red oval-shaped ball.

People swarmed around the foodstalls and rummaged through the items in the 'back of a ute' sale. They oohed and ahhed at the display of Shady Creek Riding Club's ribbons, trophies and photos, and they riffled through the pre-loved clothing stall that Mrs Cho was running. Flea had managed to organize a signed football guernsey in a frame for the silent auction and people were taking turns to scribble down their bids on pieces of paper and push them through a slot into a box. The guernsey was black and red and was causing a lot of excitement. Becky had thought of everything and I'd never been so proud to be her best friend.

And now she was trusting me to ride her horse.

I felt so good on Charlie's back, so alive, so real. I rubbed my fingers into the bay gelding's mane and breathed in his smell. I knew that this, this feeling, was all I wanted. I could live without being Prime Minister or being famous or being the most popular girl in school. I could live without chocolate or fancy private schools or winning ribbons. But I could never live without horses. I could never live without how much I loved Honey and the way she trusted me. I could never live without how I felt when I was riding, how my horse and I were one, with one heart and one spirit.

I had the answer to my question.

I belonged on horseback.

No matter where I was, as long as I was on horseback I was home.

Charlie was warmed up and we were ready. The crowd were clinging to the fence around the arena, watching us intently. Three empty red-and-white drums, lids on, were set up in the three points of a triangle. There were about ten metres between each drum. I couldn't wait to get out there, bending and twisting and galloping, trying to beat my best-ever time.

I'd been barrel racing for so long. Holly had taught me first and it had become the mounted game I loved best. I knew the routine like it was written on my heart. Straight down to the first barrel, the tip of the triangle, then around it to my left and a loop around the second barrel. As fast as we could to the third barrel and one last loop then a scramble back to the start.

Becky was speaking into the megaphone. One minute to go. Pree was ready to time me. Beck had organized a guessing competition and Em was selling tickets — one dollar for three guesses of how many seconds it would take me to finish the course.

A jar of lollies would be awarded to the winner. Pree held it up and kids wrapped themselves around her waist. She had a silver whistle around her neck and it flashed like a mirror in the sunlight.

Thirty seconds to go.

I gathered my reins. My stirrups were long, so that I could sit deep in the saddle. I leaned forward ever so slightly and fixed my eyes on the first barrel. Charlie was ready. His ears flicked backwards, telling me he knew I was there and that he was listening to me.

'Good gir — uh — boy,' I said. 'Good boy.' I wasn't used to saying it. I'd been riding mares for years now. Pepper, my first horse at South Beach, had been a gelding but that had been a long time ago.

Ten seconds. Nine. Eight.

I licked my lips.

Seven. Six. Five.

Charlie stamped his foot and held his head up high.

Four. Three. Two.

I held tight to the reins and waited.

One.

Pree blew the whistle.

I squeezed my legs and Charlie needed no more. He stretched out into a gallop. His feet pounded against the earth. I stared at the barrel. It was the only thing standing between us and barrel racing history and I had to defeat it.

We neared the barrel and I sat deep, pulling Charlie's nose into it with my hands and pushing him towards it with my legs and seat. He slowed as we rounded the barrel. Charlie twisted his body around it and stretched out again.

We galloped towards the next barrel. It loomed ahead. I was vaguely aware of the shouts of the crowd, all hoping that I'd make it to the finish line in the same number of seconds that they'd guessed. They were like a blur of colour and noise. As usual when I was riding, everything else disappeared. It was just me and the horse and the delicious, delectable dash towards the finish line.

Charlie's nose was close to the second barrel. He rounded it and I leaned in towards it, so close I could touch it. I sat deep as we galloped away. One more to go.

I applied pressure to Charlie's mouth with my hands and to his sides with my legs and he slowed as we twisted around the last barrel. Then I let him have his head and we thundered home to the roar of the crowd.

I pulled Charlie up and rubbed his neck.

'Good boy,' I murmured. 'Good boy.'

His ears flicked back to the sound of my voice. I dismounted and hugged his neck, kissing the side of his face.

Pree grabbed the megaphone from Becky and announced my time — thirty-one seconds! A girl wearing a red-and-white football guernsey and a pair of jeans whoo-hooed and jumped up and down, then rushed to Pree to claim her lolly jar prize.

I felt incredible, amazing, on fire! I loosened Charlie's girth and raised his stirrups. When we left the arena, little kids swarmed around us, clapping. A girl asked me to autograph her pamphlet and told me she wanted to ride like me. It was awesome. Better than awesome. Emily rushed over and threw her arms around my neck.

'You were so good!' she cried. 'I've never seen anything like it. You rocked!'

After a while my higher-than-a-kite feeling and Toffee's spectacular soccer display were over and so was the Open Day. There was nothing more to do but clean up and count our money. I was dying to know how much we had raised for our polocrosse team. How much Becky had raised. She'd done all the hard work and she so deserved the credit.

Two hours of cleaning and packing (and only four packets of lamingtons to get rid of) later, we'd counted $2,374.55! Beck, Pree, Em and I were gobsmacked. We sat together on a log.

'Let's celebrate,' Em said, reaching for a six-pack of lammies.

'I never thought we'd make that much,' Becky said. 'That garlic naan was something else by the way.'

'Made by my very own hands.' Pree grinned and winked. 'Taste tested by them, anyway.'

'Beck, you're a legend,' I said, breaking a lammie in half. No matter how many I'd eaten over the last twenty-four hours they were so so good.

'You raised heaps,' Em said. She took a huge bite out of a lamington and sighed, sending desiccated coconut flying. 'I tell you, I've got such a sore bottom. I think I must've ridden at least twenty-five ponies today.'

'More like five ponies five times each!' Pree giggled. 'What're you gonna spend the money on, Becky?'

Becky held a lammie in one hand and counted fingers with the other. 'Polocrosse uniforms, sticks, balls and membership fees. And you'll be pleased to know we got fourteen new members. They signed up, paid and everything.'

I clinked lammies with her. 'Well done!'

The day had been amazing. Becky had worked so hard and I was so proud of her. The club was looking healthier than it had in ages and the Shady Creek riders were starting to show the first symptoms of polocrosse fever. And most awesome of all, I'd spent the day with my best friends. We sat together and watched as the last of the Open Day was packed up around us and knew that life didn't get much better than this.

eighteen

A Portrait of the Artist

'Where've you been?' I glowered at Claire as she walked into our room. She had an overnight bag slung over her shoulder.

Claire sniffed. 'Exeat. Like you. Where d'you think? I have a family, remember?' Claire dropped her bag on the floor, scuttled to her desk and began counting her books. They were all neatly arranged in height order, tallest books on the left descending to smallest on the right. Sometimes I rearranged one or two of them, just to see how she'd react.

'Why d'you board? You live in town.'

Claire pushed a ruler against her books, making sure they were lined up in a straight row, and cast a glance at my own desk. It looked like a huge tossed book salad with a nice dressing of pencil cases, papers and plastic knick-knacks. 'It's just the way it is.'

I knew that Claire was the only local girl who boarded. All the rest were day girls, including Ricki. Why did it have to be different for Claire? I knew it must be terrible for her to be surrounded by memories of her brother. But didn't her mum miss her? Wouldn't she have wanted to hold her and never let her go? I thought about my own mum.

'How long've you been a boarder?' No matter what I'd heard about cats my whole life, I was gripped with curiosity.

'Since Year Five,' Claire said. 'Since as soon as they started taking boarders. I was the only Year Fiver in the whole boarding house. You're the first roommate I've ever had.' She gave me a look. One of those squinty, suspicious looks. 'What d'you wanna know for?'

'No reason,' I said casually. 'Ever had to share a room at home?'

Claire shook her head. 'Never. There's only me at home now.'

I knew why, but I didn't say anything.

'Are you an only child?' I said. My heart started to thump. I so wanted her to tell me.

Claire's face flushed. 'I really don't wanna talk about it,' she grouched.

'Oh,' I said, stung. I was only trying to help, only trying to get to know her. I marched towards the door. Somewhere in the kitchen there was a mug of hot chocolate and a bikkie with my name on it. I tripped over Claire's bag and a thick book fell out of it and onto the floor. I picked it up and it flipped open to an amazing drawing of a boy's face. It was in pencil. I didn't know much about art, but from the look of it Claire had used shading and delicate lines with a whole range of different leads. It was beautiful. I turned the page. There was another drawing. It was the same boy. He was smiling. I turned another page, then another and another.

'Hey!' Claire cried. She bounded across the room, snapped the book closed and snatched it from me, then held it against her chest. 'What d'you think you're doing? You shouldn't be looking at this. It's mine!'

'Did you do those?' I said. 'They're amazing! You could be a professional. Ever thought about it?' I pointed to the book. 'Who's the boy, anyway?'

'Shut up, okay!' Claire's eyes were wild. 'And mind your own business.'

'But who's the boy?' I knew. But I wanted her to say it out loud. If she would only talk about Cameron, I knew she'd start to feel better. It had been the same for me when I'd had the dreaded tingles. When I'd kept the secret of my fears locked away inside my heart, they ate away at it. Once I'd started talking, the fears had lost their power.

'Will you get out?' Claire shrieked. She yanked the door of our room open.

'I'm sorry, okay!' I stood where I was, determined that I wasn't going anywhere.

'Leave me alone!' Claire cried.

'No.' I folded my arms and stared at her.

Claire watched me with wide eyes. Her bushy dark hair was almost standing on end. She was breathing hard. 'No one has ever seen my book. It's mine. It's private.'

'I promise I won't say anything,' I said. Claire seemed to deflate a little, relieved. 'If you tell me who he is.'

Claire's mouth opened but she said nothing. We looked at each other for a few moments, just long enough for me to know what uncomfortable silences are all about. Then she sat at her neat-as-a-furniture-catalogue desk. She took a slim tin pencil case from the top drawer, then flipped open to a fresh new page in her book and started drawing.

I stood behind her. 'What're you drawing?'

She shook her head, saying nothing, only drawing. Before long the shades and lines became a face. A face that looked a lot like Claire's.

'Is it Cameron?' I said. My voice was barely a whisper.

Claire hiccupped and nodded and began to cry, but she didn't stop drawing. I didn't know whether to touch her or not so I just stood beside her and told her everything would be all right.

'It won't,' she said. 'Things will never be all right. How can they be when he's ...' Claire dropped her pencil and buried her face in her hands, sobbing hard. 'It was my fault. It was all my fault.'

'It was an accident,' I said softly. 'It wasn't your fault.'

Claire shook her head again. 'You just don't get anything, do you? It was my ... the ... it was my horse!'

Shock seeped from the top of my head to my toes, leaving me cold. Everything, every piece of the puzzle snapped instantly into place. My first impulse was to ask her what had happened to the horse, to ask why Cameron was riding it, but I said nothing. I sat on my bed and watched her cry and really didn't know what to do.

'D'you want me to get Miss Stephens?' I said at last. I'd wanted this. But now that it was here I was scared.

'What for?' Claire uncovered her face. 'Nothing she can say will bring him back, will it?'

'No,' I said. 'I guess not.'

Claire picked up her pencil again. She held it against the page and traced it gently over Cameron's chin. 'He was my brother.'

'I'm so sorry, Claire.' I touched the photo of Jason that I had stuck on the wall beside my bed with sticky tape.

'I can't live with the horses, Ashleigh,' she said. 'Not anymore.'

I pulled my pyjamas out from under my pillow. 'I can't live without them.'

Claire put down her pencil. She looked into my eyes and for the first time I saw who she really was. I saw beyond the germs and dirt phobia, the anti-horsism, the snoring and everything else that had driven me crazy about Claire. I saw that she was hurt and lonely and very scared. 'I guess it's war then.' She spoke softly like she didn't want to say the words at all.

I dragged my T-shirt over my head and tossed it on the floor, then put on my pyjamas. 'It doesn't have to be.'

Claire shrugged. 'My brother's dead. I hate horses. My family's a mess. I have no friends. Let's face it …' Claire took a deep breath and sighed. 'I've got nothing left to lose.'

I shook my head. 'You're wrong.'

'About which part?' Claire walked over to her bed and changed into her pyjamas.

'About friends. You've got a new friend in me.'

Claire ripped back the sheets and flopped down, then pulled the sheets up tight under her chin and sighed again. 'That's nice. I still hate horses, but.'

Call me crazy but I wanted to be her friend. I was never going to let her win, though. The horses were staying at Linley. There was room for them, for me and for her. There was room for everyone.

'You ready to ride?' Demi James smiled up at me. It was group riding lesson time and I was psyched. I grinned back at her from my saddle.

I'd gone to see Demi when I'd heard about Lightning. Even now, I was still in shock. Imagining him in the yard, imagining his beautiful body lying motionless after the injection, imagining that he were Honey, that it was my horse in danger … I couldn't bear to think about it.

I'd told Demi that it hadn't been Lightning's fault or hers. I told her that I accepted responsibility and that I'd told Mrs Freeman the same. I told her that I was going to do whatever it took to save the riding program and Lightning and I could tell she knew I meant it.

'Yes,' I said. 'Definitely yes.'

'Excellent!' Demi set about inspecting the girls' tack.

Levels A and B were mounted and warming up in the indoor arena. India was still the only A level. I had a deep and very meaningful conversation with myself. I was going to ride my heart out today. I was going to show India and Demi and everyone else in that arena that I deserved to be in A level too. Whatever Demi threw at me, I promised myself that I would ride through it, no matter what.

Demi barked her usual warm-up routine at us from the centre of the arena. She was Cougar-less. It was the best way, she'd explained, to move between students. I concentrated hard. Honey was willing and responsive.

I cantered her clockwise around the arena on the outside track, keeping about six or so horse lengths between Honey and the rider in front. Honey's steps were smooth, even, rhythmical. Her feet pounded against the arena floor. I looked ahead, through her ears, moving my body along with hers, fusing myself to this horse, this creature with her own will and her own mind who had allowed me into her world and onto her back. My body soaked up every move of hers.

As I rode I thought about my seat. I'd been instructed a thousand times, two thousand even, on the correct seat. I tried to keep my back straight. I sat on my seat bones, not on my bottom, pushing my hip joints slightly forward. My legs were down, but I wasn't pushing down into my heels. I rested the broadest part of my feet on the stirrups. I pointed my toes forward and held my elbows at my hips.

It was a challenge. Keeping my body in this unnatural position had taken a long time to learn and took thinking about. It was tiring and there were rules that couldn't be broken. But it helped me to be a better rider and to be as one with my horse. So no matter how sore and how tired I'd feel when I lay in bed that night, I knew it would all be worth it.

'Ashleigh, keep riding and listen,' Demi's voice called across the arena. 'Your seat's technically perfect.'

So it should be, I thought. After all those lessons!

'There's only one element missing,' she continued. 'You're technically perfect, but there's something more I want from you. I want that face relaxed for a start, you're not in trouble. I want you to begin your thought processes from your tummy, not from your head. Your tummy is your centre, the centre of your body. If you can shift your awareness from your head to your centre you'll feel more connected to your horse, more balanced.'

I thought about what she had said. I tried to pull my awareness from my head to my centre. I tried to ride from my tummy. I understood what Demi meant, but all I ended up with was a cramp. It was something I was going to need to practise.

Warm-up was finished and the level A's and B's halted their mounts and lined up. I felt calm and content. There was nothing like riding my Honey horse in a steady even canter to make me feel like the world was turning as it should. Honey was fit, warm and ready, and I was ready too.

Demi stood in front of us. She had a big red canvas bag at her feet. 'Horseball.'

I stared at her. 'Pardon?'

'Horseball,' she repeated. 'Anyone ever heard of it before?'

The class erupted.

'Are you talking about those playing balls horses have in their stables to keep them from going crazy?'

'No, it's those licking things you hang up in a stall.'

'You don't even wanna know what I'm thinking!'

'I don't even know what you're talking about.' India glowered at Demi.

Demi raised her eyebrows. 'Has anyone ever heard of it before?'

I shot up my hand. I hated looking like a know-all, but I hated keeping horsy information to myself even more. I couldn't help it. If I knew the answer, it just burst out of me. 'Maybe.'

'Tell me what you know.' For the first time in a long time, Demi looked eager to hear what I had to say.

'It's a bit like basketball on horseback,' I said. I could feel every single eye on me. One pair of eyes was doing its very best to bore holes into the side of my head. 'You score goals by throwing a ball through a hoop.'

'Right!' Demi smiled and pulled a strange-looking ball out of the canvas bag. It was like a soccer ball with leather straps attached to it. 'All you need to play horseball is a ball like this, a good balanced seat, a horse or pony and a net.'

Demi passed the ball to India, who held it at arm's length, like she was holding a baby with a pooey nappy, and inspected it. Karina raised her hand. 'What kind of net?'

Demi looked up at the ceiling, deep-thought-style. 'It looks like a basketball net that's been sewn up at the end and then turned on its side to face the playing field. The pole it's fixed to is a bit taller than a basketball pole. The hoop is about a metre wide and the net extends to about a metre and a half and holds the ball after a goal is scored.'

'Why are we talking about horseball?' Janie raised her hand and India handed the ball over to Karina.

'I'd really like to introduce it here at Linley as an alternative to polocrosse and to improve riding skills.

For those of you who play polocrosse it can only help your game. It's not played much in Australia right now, but I've played it overseas and it's heaps of fun. I think we could start something really big, and we need some good horse publicity.'

My face burned with shame and I stared at my hands. Now I understood what she was trying to do. There was so much pressure to close the riding program that Demi was desperate for a new sport that would attract more riders and save the horses. Karina kicked at my foot and I gave her a look. She passed me the ball and I held it for a moment. It didn't just look like a soccer ball, it was a soccer ball. It was white with light blue patches and was surrounded by a harness which had six leather handles attached to it. Each handle looked to be about as long as a school ruler from end to end. It looked a bit like Saturn with wonky rings. Janie cleared her throat loudly and I passed her the ball.

'It's a pretty safe sport and quite horse-friendly, though I'd recommend wearing kneepads — you'll probably end up knocking knees with other riders,' Demi said. 'Some people in the UK and France call it "rugby on horseback", but it's really a mix of rugby and basketball, like Ashleigh said before.'

I looked at Demi cautiously. She gave me a small wink and I felt instantly relieved. I knew then I wanted to do whatever I could to help get horseball off the ground. If it would make her happy, make amends and help the riding program, I'd do whatever I had to.

'First things first, though,' Demi said, shoving the ball back into the bag. 'And the most important first thing in horseball is balance. When you catch the ball you have to drop your reins and the ball must pass to each of the three riders on the team before they can shoot for a goal. Basically you'll spend a lot of time without your reins and relying on your seat and legs. And then there's picking up the ball.'

'No sticks!' I gasped.

'Right again,' Demi said. She was enthusiastic. But then again, it wouldn't be her riding around an arena with five others, no reins and no stick! 'Riders have to lean over in the saddle and scoop the ball up off the ground if it's dropped, so again, seats and legs!'

'No one can pick up a ball from the saddle,' India scoffed. 'It's impossible.'

'In horseball the stirrups are tied together under the horse's belly with a pick-up strap so you can reach down without falling. You can get them specially made, but a spare stirrup leather works just as well. And the handles on the ball help, too.'

'Can we play now? Today?' I had a dream. Already! I'd be the first-ever captain of an Australian horseball team. We'd compete in England or France or maybe America. And for the first time ever, Australia would win!

'We need to train first. You need to learn the rules. It might be a good idea to study some horseball DVDs. Remember, not only will this game be totally new to you, it'll also be totally new to your horses. Most of them are used to the close contact and speed of polocrosse, but they'll need to learn to accept a larger ball flying around.'

'Anything else?' India was surly.

'Yes. You'll need to learn to live without reins.'

In no time Demi had us riding at a walk, clockwise around the arena. 'Use your seat! Use your legs. Your seat should be glued to that saddle. Sit deep!'

The horses were turning right. I knew what I had to do. I held my reins, my hands following the movement of Honey's neck. My inside hand opened outwards to bend her neck to the right, my outside hand controlled how far she could bend. My legs kept a gentle pressure on her sides. My outside leg was behind the girth, bending her quarters around my inside leg which was on the girth. I leaned a little to the right using my seat.

'Good.' Demi was watching us carefully. 'Now drop your reins. But hold your hands like you would normally — like you're still holding your reins. Don't change too much for your horse at once.'

I knew Honey. I trusted her. I trusted my seat and legs. I dropped my reins.

We walked around the arena for a lap. I was so used to using my hands I almost had to sit on them to control the urge to pick up my reins. But we did it!

Demi asked us for a trot, rising or sitting, whichever we were most comfortable with. I chose to sit for the trot and asked Honey with my legs. She responded and I remained sitting deep, as I had for the walk, allowing my tummy to absorb the movement of her body. I tried to stay relaxed and keep my legs long, and I especially tried to remember to breathe. I held my hands where they would have been if I'd had my reins. We trotted one lap, then another and another, all without reins!

'Excellent, Ashleigh!' Demi called. 'Now I want you to stand in your stirrups. There'll be plenty of horseball games where you'll be on your feet, shooting a ball at the goal without your reins. Start to learn balance now!'

I snuck a look at her. Was she crazy? Demi's dark eyes were serious. Her black eyebrows were knotted together. I took a deep breath and stood. Honey's ears flicked back, like she was asking me just what do you think you're doing, but she kept trotting.

'Good girl!' I cried. I held my arms out for a moment, to keep my balance, then sat back down and picked up my reins. I moved Honey to the inside track, where I could walk safely, then halted her near Demi and dismounted.

'How was that?' Demi asked. She rubbed Honey's neck. 'She's a good girl.'

'Awesome,' I gushed. 'It really was. I can't wait to start training.'

'Cool her out. And welcome to level A.' Demi gave me a smile and turned back to the class.

I punched the air. I'd made it to level A! We'd both worked so hard, my Honey horse and me, and we'd done it!

nineteen

Hot Seat

The second-last week of term was going to be huge. The whole school (except Year Twelve) had half-yearly exams. I wasn't looking forward to them one little bit. I had a hunch I might go okay in Horsemanship, but Music, Maths and History were write-offs and I'd abandoned hope of ever being a Latin scholar in the second week of first term. While the rest of the class had been happily conjugating verbs for months, I was still stumped by what conjugations actually were.

The last day of exams was Thursday and a huge meeting had been planned for that evening — the perfect way to unwind after a week of torture! Word about Lightning's fate had got out and the

Board had been swamped with complaints. Nobody could understand why, if the victim (i.e., me!) was totally opposed to him being destroyed, President Carlson was so keen? I had a fair idea, but President Carlson had to be made to understand. Lightning hadn't been the one. It had been Claire's horse and no matter what she did or how many horses were put at risk or whether the riding program was closed or not, not one of those things, nothing at all in fact, would ever bring Cameron back. Mrs Freeman had approved one last meeting and it was expected to be explosive.

On top of all that, Maryanne, still shell-shocked from our thumping at the last polocrosse game, had organized a training session every day after school. She was insisting that I ride Honey in the next match but my gorgeous mare needed so much more time. I was exhausted just thinking about it.

Regular classes were cancelled and exams had been scheduled. We had two exams a day. There was a morning session from nine until eleven, a lunch and study break, then an afternoon session from one until three. By the end of day one (Monday — English in the morning and Latin in the afternoon) I felt like the teachers of Linley had done unto my brain what the Ancient Egyptian mummifiers had done unto the brains of the Pharaohs. It was a horrible process that involved nostrils, a long thin hook, squishing and liquifying and I squirmed whenever I thought about it.

Monday afternoon's polocrosse training session started at four. India was there on Rusty, practising throwing the ball to Cleo. Sarah and Stephanie were teamed up, Sarah trying to throw for goal and Stephanie desperately defending it. I was paired up with Katie.

'How long is this session?' Katie groaned as Maryanne cantered past.

'As long as it takes.' Cav halted and Maryanne watched us. 'You two are supposed to be working on your scooping. Why are you just sitting there?'

Katie's face darkened. 'It's exams, Mare. Just coz you don't have any doesn't mean we don't. If I fail this term my parents'll put me up for sale.'

Maryanne laughed. 'You know they won't. And I've done plenty of sessions when I've had exams and assessments and you didn't.'

Maryanne turned Cavvy towards India and Cleo and trotted away. Katie rolled her eyes. 'Man. She's totally a dictator.'

'She's awesome!' I said. 'Let's get into it.'

Katie gathered her reins in one hand and sighed. 'It's only my school certificate, right?'

'Right!' I grinned. 'Next year.'

Katie laughed. 'Get scooping, kid.'

Katie flicked her stick towards me and the ball landed on the ground a few metres away. I applied pressure to Honey's sides and she sprang into a canter. I leaned forward and to my right and scooped. I had the ball in my net then I flicked and Katie cantered forward and scooped. We practised over and over and over until we were both exhausted and exhilarated at the same time. Best of all, it was so good to be practising on Honey.

The meeting was starting to look like a natural disaster. I knew it was coming. It had been forecast. I'd locked my doors, taped down my windows and gathered enough stones to spell out SOS, but no amount of cyclone preparation was going to make it any less unpleasant to be caught right in the eye of the storm. Now that I knew about Claire's brother, Cameron, I was dreading it even more. I was ready to fight to the death for the horses, but knowing that Claire was fighting to kill her guilt, grief and confusion was going to make it so much harder to stand up and make my speech.

The assembly hall was full to bursting. There were more parents, more girls and more staff than at any other meeting. Even reporters from the local paper had managed to squeeze inside. It seemed that the whole school, the whole town, the whole horsy universe even, were as desperate to know the fate of the Linley riding program as I was. But it wasn't just the program. It was Lightning, too.

I sat on the stage shaking, scanning the faces for Em and Ricki. I thought I spotted them once or twice but gave up in the end and ran my eyes over my speech. I'd typed it up and made the font so large I was sure each word could be picked up by a satellite. I'd tried to memorize it. But I was so scared up there, with all those eyes watching me, that I could barely remember which direction to sit on a horse. My tummy churned and the tingles were making my heart feel like it had been stuffed into a washing machine with the knob stuck on spin. It wasn't nice at all.

Finally Mrs Freeman called the meeting to order. She introduced the speakers then President Carlson stood up. She went on and on about the dangers of horses and riding. After listening to what she'd said at the last meeting, I'd wanted to fill her car with a cartload of fresh Honey poo. But now that I knew her story, I wasn't as angry with her. I didn't necessarily like her, and I still hated what she said and could never agree with her. But I understood her so much more. As she spoke I watched her hands. She was hanging on tight to the podium. I imagined her hands holding her baby boy and felt sick inside to see them empty as she left the podium.

I stood on wobbly legs. Each step towards the podium seemed to take a week. By the time I was holding onto the podium I felt like I'd been walking for a year. Someone burst from nowhere it seemed and adjusted the microphone so that it was right in front of my face. I spread out my speech (which was now starting to look a little like origami) and cleared my throat.

'Good evening.' I tried to smile. Em had told me to look confident and project my voice, but the only thing I thought I might be about to project was going to be coming from my tummy and not my voicebox. And it had a good chance of covering everyone sitting in the first five rows. 'I'm Ashleigh Miller. You might know me if you were at the last meeting. But if you don't, there's something you should know about me that's very very important.

'I'm a horse lover. And it's my dream to ride for Australia one day. I hope I make it. I may not, but I really want to try and I'll do everything and give anything to make my dream come true.' I cleared my throat again and tried to calm my nerves by imagining every member of the audience in their underwear — bad image! Very bad image, indeed. 'I know that Linley will play a huge part in chasing and living my dream, and even though it has some risks, dreams usually won't come true without a little daring.'

A few people clapped. I caught a glimpse of Em and Ricki at last. They were both grinning like maniacs and giving me the thumbs up. I smiled at last, for real, feeling something like electricity running into my heart.

'When we think about dreamers we only need to look at the women here, behind me.' I pointed at the portraits of Vicki Roycroft, Dame Enid Lyons and Evonne Goolagong Cawley, three truly remarkable, incredible Australian women who made me so proud. 'What if they hadn't dreamed? What if the Romans hadn't dreamed or the Greeks or the

Egyptians? What if writers didn't dare to write or artists didn't dare to paint or athletes didn't dare to train and compete and try to win? What would be the point of anything at all without dreams?'

I was starting to feel a little better about being up on stage. It was like all the passion I felt for the words I'd written and the beautiful creatures that had inspired them was filling my heart with fire. 'Sure,' I continued, 'riding can be dangerous. But the real danger is in not trying to understand the horse or listen to what they're telling you. It's also in doing silly things. The challenge was silly and it hurt more people than I ever imagined. It was my fault and I'm sorry. Please keep the riding program going, it's there to teach us to be safe around horses. And please don't take my dream away from me. It's me that's chosen it, or perhaps it chose me. If it's not for you, walk away. But for those of us here at Linley Heights who share my dream, leave us to follow it. Allow us to fly.'

The hall was silent for a moment. I gathered my piece of paper and turned back to my seat. Suddenly the hall erupted. Girls were on their feet, yelling and cheering and clapping. Most of the parents joined in. I stole a look at President Carlson. It was clear what Linley wanted. She sighed and slumped in her chair.

'Thank you.' My throat tightened up and my eyes stung and I knew I was going to cry. No matter how I tried to stop them it was no use. The tears spilled down my face. I was so relieved it was over but so terribly sad for the Carlsons all at once. Just when I thought I couldn't take it anymore, a man wearing a cowboy hat stepped up onto the stage and introduced himself to the audience as Sebastian Samuels, Secretary of the Parents' Association. I was shocked. Ricki looked proud. The smile on her face was huge and her eyes were wide. She stared up at her dad. I stared at him too.

Mr Samuels thanked everyone for attending and announced that due to overwhelming support for the riding program, the matter would now be put to rest. He assured us that the Parents' Association would withdraw its petition to the Board to end the riding program and have Lightning destroyed, and that the school body would be officially notified of the same by letter in the next few days. He thanked President Carlson and me for speaking and thanked Mrs Freeman. Then he did something I never expected.

He walked across the stage and held his hand out to President Carlson. She stood and smoothed down her skirt and then her hair, cleared her throat and shook hands. I knew right away what he was doing. He was allowing her to be defeated gracefully. He leaned in and said something to President Carlson that made her cover her eyes with her hand and nod. She pulled a tissue from the pocket of her jacket and dabbed at her nose. She sat down again and he gently patted her shoulder, then took to the podium once more.

'We're all different,' Mr Samuels said. 'There are those of us who have horses in our blood, and those of us who just don't. And there are those of us who've been battered somewhat by life and are trying to find our way to healing. But there's room enough for everyone at Linley Heights and that, apart from anything else, is what makes this school so great.'

Mr Samuels thanked the audience again and wished everyone a good night. President Carlson shook hands with Mrs Freeman, and the hall emptied of people and noise and it was all over.

I'd done it. Lightning was safe. Demi was over the moon. The horses were staying. I'd done it and I couldn't have asked for anything else.

'This is it, girls.' Maryanne James paced. We lined up in front of her and I sent my most sincere (and desperate) prayers to the horse gods. *Let us win. Please, please, please, let us win.* We were playing the pink-shirts, Wallaby Hill, our very favourite opponents. They weren't our favourites because we loved to play them. They were our favourites because we wanted to beat them. They'd beaten us once already this season. They had attitude and we Linley girls were hungry to knock it out of them.

'Our last game this term. And after our loss to St Andrew's—'

'Don't remind me,' muttered Stephanie.

'I don't like reminding myself.' Maryanne frowned. 'As I was saying, after our loss to St Andrew's we have a lot to prove. Some people have been saying that they beat us coz they have three boys on their team. I say that's garbage. I say we could beat an all-boy team even if we were blindfolded, had broken sticks and were riding chihuahuas!'

'Go, Mare! Go, Mare!' Cleo chanted, dancing in her saddle.

'So let's get out there and show 'em what Linley girls can do!'

'Whoo, whoo, whoo!' screeched Sarah as our first team rode out onto the field. India, Katie and Stephanie had been teamed up. India was the Number Two (the centre) again (it had been my turn to make a dumb number two joke and I'd really enjoyed it), Katie was the goal scorer — Number One — and Steph was Number Three. In my team, I was Number Three, and charged with defending our goal.

I loved the way we were trained to play any position in polocrosse. In footy, if you were a forward you were a forward. In netball, if you were a centre you were a centre. In polocrosse you could be anybody and take on anyone. It was the most awesome game I'd ever played. I wondered if horseball would even compare. But hey, it was a horse sport. What else mattered? I'd already seen a few DVDs and clips on the Internet and, from the look of it, horseball rocked and I couldn't wait to start training next term!

Linley Juniors looked cool in their white joddies, black boots, dark navy polo shirts and white helmets. I was proud as a Melbourne Cup winner sitting on my Honey horse's back on the sidelines, watching as India flicked the ball to Katie who sent it, *zoom*, into the Wallaby Hill goal. I roared with disgust as the Wallaby Hill Number Two charged her huge bay gelding into Caramel's shoulder, sending him sprawling. I gasped and slapped my hands over my mouth when Stephanie tumbled from the saddle and narrowly missed being trampled by Chops. I felt like part of the team and part of the school and couldn't wait to be out there.

The horn blasted and the chukka was over.

'You were amazing!' I cried as India, Katie and Steph trotted from the field. At that moment I didn't care how humungous a jerkette India was. She was my partner in polocrosse and she'd played really well. The score was three–nil, Linley's way, and we were pumped.

My team took to the field at last. It was the first time Honey had played a match, but I had faith in her. We'd trained hard and I'd given her a little talking-to, which had involved a few blasts of the air horn, letting her sniff it and rubbing it over her body. By the time our woman-to-woman chat was over Honey wasn't even flinching at the horn.

The umpire threw in the ball. I turned Honey

and charged towards our goal, right through the pack of horses, scattering them while their riders scrambled for the ball.

'You moron!' a Wallaby Hill girl screeched and was promptly warned by the umpire. The Wallabies were unsettled and Linley snatched the ball.

Sarah had it in her racquet. 'Cleo, get ready!'

Cleo held her stick high. 'Here. HERE!'

Sarah flicked the ball and Cleo caught it. No matter how many times I saw someone take a catch in polocrosse it amazed me. Riding at a canter and sometimes a gallop, one-handed, catching a small ball in a small net! Wow!

Cleo flung the ball at the undefended goal and it sailed through. Linley roared and I wanted to scream in delight.

The ball was thrown in again. It was close, so close. I reached forward and scooped it up, then turned Honey and tore away from the pack. Two Wallabies followed me, thinking they'd figured me out. I was flanked by hot pink and in danger of being sandwiched, which would force me to throw the ball and potentially lose it. I held tight to my stick and demanded a halt from Honey. She skidded,

Western Sliding–Halt style (I was chuffed beyond chuffed that she'd finally done it — all that Western training had paid off after all) and the Wallabies lost control of me. By the time they'd realized what I'd done I'd flicked the ball to Cleo who sent it roaring through the goal, securing us another goal and in the end a thirteen–seven win over the pinks.

The Linley crowd were on their feet. I could see Maryanne and Demi on the sidelines jumping up and down and screaming and felt that no matter what the final score was, Honey and I had proved to everyone that we were part of the team, part of Linley and that nothing and no one could ever take that away from us.

twenty

Bridle Path

'You look amazing!'

I stared at Jenna. She looked the most beautiful I'd ever seen her. Her short blonde hair was pinned up on top of her head like a halo, making her blue eyes look huge. She had silver sparkles on her face and glossy stuff on her lips. She wore a silver necklace with diamonds and a matching bracelet and there were diamond studs in her ears. Her dress was long and blue with silver swirls running over it, and it swished when she walked.

'I look like a dork.' Jenna scowled at her bedroom mirror. 'Everyone's gonna laugh their heads off when they see me. A bridesmaid with braces? Please!'

'Me in a dress — double please! At least your teeth match your bling.'

Jenna laughed. 'True. Wish you were coming with me, you know — in the car with me.'

I nodded. 'Me too. But that means putting the boys on the roof.'

Jenna grinned. 'Sounds good to me!'

'You need to do this with your family, Jen.' I hugged her hard. 'But I'll be right behind you the whole way.'

Jenna took a deep breath. I grabbed her hand and tugged her towards her bedroom door. It was time. Time to go to the wedding. Time to start a new life. Time to make a new family and, in a way, become a new person. She was Jenna Dawson, Josephine and Andrew's daughter, Toby's and Max's sister, Ashleigh's best friend. And after today she'd be Antonio's stepdaughter. But I understood more now. And so did she. She could be all those things, be a part of all those people's lives, and still be herself.

Josephine was waiting in the hallway. She looked so beautiful. Her hair was curled and hung down her back, and in place of a veil she wore a tiara on her head. Her white dress was silky. She held a bouquet of long-stemmed red roses in her hand.

Ant stood beside her, handsome in a new suit and shirt, holding her hand. Toby and Max ran around and around them in matching shirts, pants and ties.

'Ready, gorgeous girl?' Josephine smiled at Jenna.

'I didn't think the groom was allowed to see the bride before the wedding,' I said, my eyebrows raised.

'We've never done things the way we're supposed to.' Josephine and Antonio looked into one another's eyes. He kissed her hand and then her forehead. 'Wouldn't life be dull if everyone did what they were told?'

'I'll remember that,' Jenna said, a cheeky smile on her face.

'Me too! Me too!' Toby and Max chanted in unison.

I propelled Jenna forward, my hand on the small of her back. She linked arms with her mum and the new family walked together out of the unit and down the stairs to the car.

'I've never seen a wedding before,' I said to my mum later in our car. We were following the wedding car to the Harbour.

'That's a side-effect of being incapable of any interest outside horses.' Mum checked her lippy in the mirror. 'Can you believe this traffic, Grant?'

'As far as I'm concerned, traffic is more than two cars and one dog on the road at any one time. No wonder city folk get road rage.' Dad stroked Mum's hair. 'I wish you could sit right beside me, right here. Remember my old car with the bench seat in front? I could drive and kiss you at the same time.'

'Kiss? You guys kissed?' I fake-vomited onto my dress. 'Revolting! Can you believe this, Jase? For your own sake cover your ears.'

My baby brother screeched and grabbed his feet, clearly disgusted by their behaviour.

I peered through the gap between the two front seats. Yep. Jenna's car was still there. 'Are you sure you know where you're going? What if you lose them?'

Dad gave me a look over his shoulder. 'I lived here for thirty-eight years, Ashleigh Louise. I think I have some idea of where we're going.'

'What was your wedding like?' I grabbed Jason's foot, crammed it into my mouth and made chomping noises. He shrieked again and laughed.

'Very romantic,' Mum said. 'Until your pop made his speech. Oh, crumbs. A red light.'

'Any horses?' I blew a huge raspberry on Jason's tummy. 'Excuse yourself, young man!'

Mum turned to look at me. 'What are you talking about?'

'Pree's dad turned up to the church on a white horse. Her gran nearly died from shock. I've seen pictures. He had a huge red and gold umbrella. It was cool.'

'There were no horses anywhere in sight. You know full well that until your horse obsession kicked in, neither your father nor I had ever been anywhere near a horse in our lives. It's green. Grant, I think you missed the turn!'

'I did not miss the turn, Helen.' Dad made an odd choking noise and said something about 'back-seat drivers' that I knew I wasn't supposed to hear.

'So how come you guys are unhorsy and I'm totally horse mad?'

'Must have been that drop on the head,' Dad muttered.

'Very funny.' I took Jason's hands and made him clap. He laughed, mouth open. I could see his two top and bottom teeth. He dribbled in delight. 'I'd better drop Jase on the head, then. Make sure he turns out like me.'

'Anything but that!' Mum groaned.

I turned to look out the window. I'd forgotten how beautiful the city could be. It all seemed so incredibly big now, so busy and so new. I felt a twinge of homesickness and shook my head. What was I thinking? Shady Creek was home now. I guessed that a part of me, somewhere deep inside, would always be a city girl. It was just another piece of the jigsaw that made up who I was.

Ant had insisted on getting married somewhere by the Harbour, with the Opera House and the Bridge in the background, and they'd decided on Luna Park! It was sunny and the water was sparkling and speckled with boats.

By the time we arrived, Jenna was nowhere in sight. Neither were the boys or Josephine. Ant waited by the water's edge on the left side of an elegant dark-haired lady who was holding a golden book in her hands.

'That's the celebrant,' Mum hissed.

'You're not gonna get married again, are you?' I looked from one of my parents to the other.

Mum wrapped her arm around my shoulders. 'No. But if I did, it would be to your dad.'

'Really?' I said hopefully.

Mum sighed. 'He may not take directions very

well, but I love your dad more than anything. And I know he loves me too.'

'You mean you love him more than me? Or Jase?'

'No, I don't mean that. I love him differently. You're my daughter. Jason's my son. Grant's my husband. It's a different type of love.' Mum smiled and watched Dad toss Jason in the air. 'One day you'll understand.'

'Why do grown-ups always say that?' I grumbled. 'Why don't they just explain it so kids'll understand right away?'

'Because some things need to be learned first-hand, Ash. I can't tell you how love'll feel when it comes along. You'll just know it has and then you'll understand.' Mum kissed my cheek. She couldn't reach the top of my head anymore. 'I promise.'

I felt funny, all tight in my throat, but I nodded. 'Okay.'

Music started playing and everyone turned around. Ant looked like he was going to cry. I turned around too. Jenna was standing in a doorway, her eyes fixed on the celebrant. I saw the celebrant wave and Jenna took her first step. She held a bouquet just like her mum's. A small silk bag was looped over her wrist.

'Isn't she beautiful?' Mum gasped. 'So grown-up.'

'I know.' It was all I could say. I'd never been so proud to be her friend. Jenna walked down the aisle alone and stood beside the celebrant, on her right. She and Ant smiled at each other.

The guests 'ohhh-ed' and I looked back towards the doorway. Josephine stood flanked by her boys. She held her roses in both hands and they held on to her arms. Toby looked up and said something to his mum and she kissed his head, then Max's. For once they didn't wipe it off.

The music continued — the words, about being someone's forever, washed over me. Josephine smiled and smiled, her eyes on Ant's face. She stood in front of him and the boys nodded to one another. They took her right hand in theirs and offered it to Ant. He kissed them both and took Josephine's hand and my mum reached into her handbag for a tissue.

The wedding ceremony started. I didn't really listen to the words, I watched Jenna. I watched her face, I watched the way she tucked a wisp of her hair behind her ear, the way she held out her hand for her mum's bouquet, the way she whispered to her brothers to stand still. She was so different to the Jenna I'd known since I was five and been right through primary school with. The Jenna with the long blonde hair and the teeth that stuck out a bit and who was mad about computers. The Jenna who'd started Horse Cents with me and had riding lessons on Cassata just to please me. She was so different. And so was I in so many ways. But we were still, would always be, best friends.

'And now Josephine and Antonio will make their vows,' the celebrant said. I edged forward in my seat. Everyone was quiet and still. Even Jason shushed.

Ant and Josephine were facing each other, holding both hands. Jenna and the boys watched them.

The celebrant looked at her book. I held onto Mum's hand as Josephine and Antonio repeated their vows, including some sweet-sounding words in Italian which I didn't understand, and exchanged rings. Finally, the celebrant pronounced them husband and wife, they kissed (the boys covered their eyes) and then it was over. Josephine Dawson had become Josephine Ciciarri and the new family was official. It was time to party!

I poked at what was left of my slice of wedding cake — banana mud (Ant's favourite) — with my fork. I was full, so full I didn't know if I'd ever need to eat again. Then again, that dessert buffet looked awesome!

'Ash, guess who's here!'

I spun around, my mouth dropped open. 'Mr Dawson!'

Jenna's dad smiled. I hadn't seen him since we'd moved away. So much had happened since then, for him and for me. 'Still riding?'

'Still baking?'

He threw his head back and laughed and I laughed too. Within seconds the boys had come out of nowhere and were climbing up his legs. 'Yes, in fact. Next time you drop in I'll whip up a batch of white chocolate chunk cookies, eh?'

I nodded, realizing I had plenty of room for sweets.

'Ash, this is Michelle.' Jenna indicated a young woman with long red hair and dark brown eyes. She held out her hand and shook mine. 'It's great to meet you,' she said.

'Hi,' I said. I looked over my shoulder. Josephine and Ant were dancing together, totally oblivious. Mr Dawson, Michelle and Jenna seemed very comfortable. I was curious.

'Where's your dad, Ash? I'd love to catch up with him.' Mr Dawson peered around the room.

I pointed at a table. Dad was rocking the pram. He'd covered it in a sheet. It was time for Jason to go to bed.

'Don't forget to come and stay with us next time you're here. Jen'd love that, wouldn't you, princess?'

'Yes!' Jenna said. Mr Dawson and Michelle wandered over to Dad's table, hand in hand. 'You'll come and stay, won't you?'

'Of course! Hey, Jen — doesn't your mum mind your dad being here? I thought they didn't like each other.'

'We're staying with Dad tonight so he came to pick us up,' Jenna said matter-of-factly.

'Are you?' I was surprised.

'We all thought it was a better idea than going with Mum and Ant on their wedding night.' Jenna gave me a look.

'Fair enough,' I said quickly. It was better to end the discussion right there.

'Mum said to have some cake and Dad's cool with it. They get along, really. What's the point of all that fighting when you've got kids? Doesn't do anyone any good.' Jenna smoothed down her dress.

'Does he like Ant?'

Jenna shrugged. 'Dad's not the one who married him, is he? Anyway, Ant's a good guy and Dad knows it. Same with Mum. She's happy Dad's met Michelle.'

'Are you?' I watched her carefully.

Jenna took a moment to think. 'I wish they could've stayed married. But just coz they couldn't doesn't mean I want either of them to be alone. I mean, they have us, but only part of the time, right? It's different, I can tell you. But it's okay. And they're happy. That can't be bad.'

'What about you?'

'I'd be a whole lot happier if we were having this conversation next to the desserts!'

We wrapped an arm around each other and followed our stomachs while the bride and groom danced in slow circles in each other's arms.

twenty-one

The Final Score

'Good morrow, Ashleigh Louise!'

Dad folded me up in his arms and smooshed a big kiss on the top of my head.

I struggled to free myself, wipe off the kiss and roll my eyes at Pree at the same time. 'Dad, I think it's time you went back to work. You're getting a bit weird.'

'Surely you jest!' Dad roared, holding me at arm's length. 'Wouldst thou be interested in partaking of the midday meal?'

I raised one eyebrow. 'Have you been eating the collected works of Shakespeare recently?'

'Is this a loaf of garlic bread I see before me?

Come, let me stuff thee into my face.' Dad clutched at the air then pretended to gorge on the bread.

I shook my head slowly. 'Do you see this, Pree? What hope do I have of ever being normal with genes like this?'

Dad wrapped his arm around Pree's shoulders. 'Art thou afflicted with the pangs of hunger in thy stomach?'

Pree giggled. 'You bet. I'm so starved I could eat a bucket of aloo gobhi. It's this curry my dad makes. Hey, did I ever tell you about the time my uncle made a bet with my dad that he couldn't put away a full Indian dinner? Anyway, the rules were that he had to get it down in under an hour and then keep it down. He finished the lot then thought he was going to do this massive burp but chucked it all …'

I held up my hand. 'Thanks, Pree.'

Dad grimaced and backed into the kitchen. 'I thank-est thou for thy disgusting image, my dear. I shall get me back to mine lasagne, despite the loss-eth of my appetite.'

Pree beamed. 'You're welcome. Becky on her way?'

I nodded. 'Should be.'

Pree punched the air. 'Yes! How cool. Scrummy lunch and then an all-afternoon horse ride. Thank horse gods Honey's home. Thank horse gods Mum floated Jazz over here for me this morning. She would've collapsed if she'd had two rides in one day.'

'Your mum or Jazz?' I scowled. 'I get to have Honey home for three weeks. And the horse gods is my line by the way.'

The doorbell rang and we raced to answer it, ripping it open and laughing our heads off. We didn't stay laughing for long.

Becky was standing on the doorstep in her riding hat and braids, tears running down her face. She hiccupped loudly and wiped her nose with the back of her hand.

'What is it?' I said. My heart was thumping. Had someone been hurt? Had something happened to one of the horses?

Becky said nothing but just stood there, crying. I'd never seen her look so upset and I didn't know what to do. I thought about calling my dad but Pree grabbed Becky's hand and dragged her inside.

'What's wrong?' Pree said, unclipping Becky's helmet. She snatched a box of tissues from the reception desk.

Becky took a huge gulping breath and sighed. 'I've got, I–I've got r–really bad news.'

I rubbed her back and bit my bottom lip, wishing like crazy I had a carrot to munch on to take the nerves away. 'Tell us. Whatever it is, it can't be that bad.'

Becky began to sob, really sob. She covered her face with her hands and sat down on the floor. Pree and I gave each other a look and my tummy spun. 'It's … it's … it's Riding Club.'

My heart squeezed hard. 'What about it?'

Pree pushed some tissues into Becky's hands and she blew her nose. 'Dad just told me. He just found out this morning.'

'What the horse gods is it?' I couldn't take it anymore.

Becky wiped her eyes. 'Riding Club's over. The land's up for sale.'

'How can that be? Isn't it Gary's land?' I was confused.

Becky shook her head. 'Riding Club rents it real cheap. This old lady used to own it and she loved horses and was happy to let us stay as long as we wanted. But she died a few years ago and her kids aren't so horse crazy. Now they wanna sell.'

'Don't you have a lease? Don't you have rights?'

Becky sighed. 'I've already been through this with Dad. No lease. Only a gentleman's agreement. Well, a gentlewoman's agreement in this case.'

I was stunned. I stared at Becky. My mouth opened but I didn't know what to say.

'Selling's not so bad,' Pree said. 'Maybe the new owners'll let you stay. Maybe they'll love horses as much as we do.'

Becky shook her head. 'You don't understand. It's up for development. There are plans going in to council. The best offer'll get the land and there'll be stupid houses built all over it.'

'Oh no,' I gasped. 'What're we gonna do?'

Becky wiped her eyes again with a tissue. 'We?'

'Of course we,' Pree said. 'We're not just gonna lie down and take this, are we?'

'Not after everything we've been through. Not after everything Riding Club's meant to us!' I was feeling better. Just a little. As long as I knew that we were going to do something I felt better.

'You're right,' Becky said softly. 'Since when have we ever given up without a fight?'

'Since never!' I said, holding out my hand. 'Let's make a pact.'

'That no matter what, we'll fight to the end to save Shady Creek Riding Club!' Pree grabbed my hand, her face glowing with the excitement of cooking up an amazingly brilliant plan. 'Even though it may mean being run out of Pinebark Ridge for treachery!'

Becky laid her hand on top of ours. 'What would I do without you two?'

'You wouldn't get to share your Chinese leftovers.' Pree smacked her lips.

'And it wouldn't be three against three — you know, us versus the Creeps,' Becky said thoughtfully.

'And you wouldn't hear the best horse jokes,' I said.

'Like this one,' Pree said. 'Stop me if you've heard this one — what does it mean if you find a horseshoe? Some poor horse is walking around in his socks! D'you get it? In his socks. Coz he doesn't have his shoe!'

'That was just *so* bad!' Becky actually managed a smile.

'What's the best type of story to tell a runaway horse? A tale of WHOA! D'you get it? WHOA! As in stop, and woe!' Pree threw her head back and laughed.

Pree and I hauled Becky to her feet and we wrapped our arms around her shoulders. The three of us followed our noses to the kitchen. We had to make plans, but there was also the small matter of empty tummies that needed to be filled. Lunch was laid out for us on the table. There was a huge tray of fresh, home-made lasagne, salad and crisp bread rolls. My mouth watered.

We sat at the table and helped ourselves. Dad disappeared into reception for a while, finally able to read the telepathic messages I was sending him that parents hanging around when I had friends over was so not cool anymore.

Pree moaned suddenly. 'I've just remembered! We're gonna have some visitors.'

I gave her a look. 'No way. You can't be serious.'

Pree rolled her eyes. 'It doesn't get any more serious than Savannah and Mikenzie McMurray. They're coming for the holidays — ha!'

'Why can't we have one catastrophe at a time?'

Pree shrugged. 'Life wasn't meant to be easy for the horse mad.'

I picked up my glass of cola. 'To the horse mad!'

Becky and Pree clinked my glass with theirs. 'To the horse mad!'

I grinned and took another bite of lasagne. We would come up with a plan, I was sure of it. And no matter what we'd fight to the very end.

I curled up in bed that night, in my bed in my room. My Honey horse, reunited with Toffee, was at home safe in her own paddock, tearing at the lush green Shady Creek grass. Jason was cooing to himself in his cot, just down the hall. The guests in Room One were watching TV and Dad was fixing tomorrow's breakfast in the kitchen.

Mum knocked on my door and poked her head in. 'You awake?'

'Course,' I said. 'And why are you suddenly knocking on my door?'

Mum smiled. 'Figured I had to, now that you're a high-school girl.'

'You think I get any privacy at Linley? I get fluff in my belly button and the whole school knows about it.' I patted my bed and she sat down.

'Lemme have a look,' Mum said, tugging at my pyjama top. 'I'd hate for your routine to be disrupted.'

I slapped at her hands. 'Mum! Are you off your tree?'

Mum laughed. 'Mums are supposed to be a bit

mental. That's why we're allowed to get away with spitting on hankies and wiping our poor children's faces with them. They teach us that at Bad Mother School!'

'What's going on in here? Sounds like a party!' Dad danced into the room with Jason who grabbed handfuls of his hair and screeched. 'Got a good grip on him, this one.'

'Jase!' I held out my arms to my baby brother. I wanted to make the most of every moment I had with him before he turned into a real boy. 'D'you think he remembers me when he doesn't see me for a while?'

'You're a little hard to forget.' Mum smiled wryly.

'Gee, thanks.' I blew a raspberry on Jason's palm and he shrieked.

Mum sighed and touched my face.

'What?' I said.

'It's good to have you home, that's all. Funny, I never thought I'd ever have to deal with you leaving me. Not when you were twelve, anyway. Thought I had until you were at least thirty-five.' She grabbed my hand and kissed it.

'D'you want me to come home?' I said. I sat up and handed Jase back to Dad. 'I've wanted to so many times. Sometimes it's too hard. Sometimes I miss you … home … so much.'

Mum's eyes moistened. 'We all miss you, possum. When you're not here the house is so empty, so quiet. Sometimes I wish we just had a normal life, you know? You coming home from school in the afternoon and leaving your uniform on the floor and arguing with me about your homework. It's every mother's dream!'

I lay back on my pillow. Was it worth it? Was Linley really worth it? Sometimes I just didn't know.

Mum stood up then and kissed my forehead. 'Don't be surprised if I stand outside your door tonight. I just wanna listen to you breathe. So I know you're really here.'

I wrapped my arms around her neck and hugged her hard. My mum. I loved her and Dad and Jason so much. But I loved horses too. I wanted them both. I hugged Dad too and gave Jason one last lingering raspberry, then fell back into bed.

My first holiday at home with my Honey horse was about to begin and I had so much to do. Riding Club needed to be saved from the developers and Shady Trails needed to be saved from the McMurray girls. Bring it on!

Glossary

A4-sized paper letter-sized paper

arvo slang word for 'afternoon'

bikkie cookie (short for 'biscuit')

brumby an Australian wild or feral horse

catherine-wheel a firework that produces sparks
   and coloured flames

celebrant marriage commissioner

chook slang word for chicken

dam mare, in the sense of a horse's mother

dob (someone) in to rat them out, tell on them

dock the solid part of a horse's tail

doona comforter or quilt

exeat weekend long weekend

float horse trailer; to transport a horse by trailer

fringe bangs

guernsey jersey

maize corn

nick off get lost

Open Day open house

pong slang word for 'stink'

showbag bag of sample merchandise and other items sold at
   a fair or exhibition

troppo crazy, insane

tucker slang word for 'food'

ute a pickup truck; abbreviation for utility vehicle

verse compete against

witches' hats traffic cones, pylons

Acknowledgements

I would like to thank my publisher at HarperCollins, Lisa Berryman, my editor, Lydia Papandrea, and my agent, Jacinta di Mase, for their wonderful guidance and encouragement. To my gorgeous kids, Mariana, John and Simon — I love you and I love being your mum. To my husband, Seb — thank you for your friendship and your love, and for holding my hand through every word of *Horse Mad Whispers*. And to the readers of the series — stay horse mad!

KATHY HELIDONIOTIS lives in Sydney, Australia, and divides her time between writing stories, reading good books, teaching and looking after her three gorgeous children. Kathy has had fourteen children's books published so far. *Horse Mad Whispers* is the seventh book in the popular Horse Mad series.

Visit Kathy at her website:
www.kathyhelidoniotis.com

In the same series

ISBN 978-1-55285-952-0

Totally Horse Mad

The only things standing between Ashleigh Miller and the horse of her dreams are a whole lot of dollars that she doesn't have, parents who don't know one end of a horse from another and a city backyard the size of a shoebox. Ashleigh can't believe it when her parents announce that she will soon have a horse of her own, but at a price. She will have to say goodbye to her best friend, Jenna, South Beach Stables and her favourite horse, Princess. Ashleigh and her family are leaving the city and heading for Shady Creek, a small country town.

ISBN 978-1-55285-953-7

Horse Mad Summer

Ashleigh is itching for her Horse Mad holiday with Beck and Jenna to begin. Her two best friends will be meeting each other for the first time and she's sure all three of them will have the best summer together. But when Jenna finally arrives from the city, Ashleigh feels pulled in two, torn between helping Jenna with her riding lessons and keeping an eye on the Creepketeer bullies with Becky. Then Jenna confides in Ash and makes her promise not to tell anyone — not even Becky. With the secret threatening to tear them all apart, can Ashleigh bring her two best friends together before the summer is over?

Horse Mad Academy

The Junior Cross-Country Riding Championships are over and Ashleigh Miller has arrived at Waratah Grove Riding Academy. It's a dream come true for any Horse Mad kid, but as Ashleigh discovers, reality is a different story. Training with the best junior riders in Australia, faced with a gruelling schedule and a horse who just refuses to do dressage, Ash is shocked when she finally begins to unravel Honey's mysterious past. Does she have what it takes to help her horse heal her wounds? When tensions between the riders start to run high, Ashleigh misses simpler times in Shady Creek.

Horse Mad Academy

ISBN 978-1-55285-959-9

Horse Mad Heroes

Back from Waratah Grove, Ashleigh is excited to have landed a job at Shady Trails Riding Ranch, a new riding school that has opened in Shady Creek. But rivalry between Riding Club and the ranch pits her against her best friend Becky for the first time. There's also a baby due any day now and with all the baby talk at home, Ash feels more alone than ever. When Cassata, the beautiful Appaloosa mare, goes missing, Ash and Becky are reunited. But will their quest to find Cassata be enough to mend their friendship?

Horse Mad Heroes

ISBN 978-1-55285-960-5

Horse Mad Western

Ashleigh Miller feels like she's losing control. There's her job at Shady Trails Riding Ranch, Riding Club, two horses, three best friends, three mortal enemies and two new 'friends' to take care of. With her parents' new B&B up and running, there are also guests to look after. At least there's one piece of good news in her life — Jenna is coming to visit. Meanwhile, there's the challenge of learning a whole new style of riding before the Western Riding Show. And since Gary won't own up to his past, that means taking lessons from the most experienced Western rider in Shady Creek — King Creepketeer, Flea Fowler!

Horse Mad Western

ISBN 978-1-55285-996-4

Horse Mad Heights

Ashleigh Miller has landed a riding scholarship to the prestigious Linley Heights School and she's on top of the world. What horse-mad kid wouldn't want to live, learn and ride at a school where the riding arena is the classroom, the teachers wear joddies and your horse can board with you? It's hard being the new kid, though, what with strict school rules, revolting food and a cranky dorm mate. Then a bully pushes Ash's buttons, and the stakes rise. Is being totally horse mad enough to help Ash survive at Linley Heights — or will it be her demise?

Horse Mad Heights

by Kathy Helidoniotis

ISBN 978-1-55285-997-1